BITTER
LEMONS

by

Neil Doloughan

Grosvenor House
Publishing Limited

All rights reserved
Copyright © Neil Doloughan, 2015

The right of Neil Doloughan to be identified as the author of this
work has been asserted in accordance with Section 78
of the Copyright, Designs and Patents Act 1988

The book cover picture is copyright to Neil Doloughan

This book is published by
Grosvenor House Publishing Ltd
28-30 High Street, Guildford, Surrey, GU1 3EL.
www.grosvenorhousepublishing.co.uk

This book is sold subject to the conditions that it shall not, by way of
trade or otherwise, be lent, resold, hired out or otherwise circulated
without the author's or publisher's prior consent in any form of binding or
cover other than that in which it is published and
without a similar condition including this condition being imposed
on the subsequent purchaser.

This is a book of fiction. Most of the locations named exist, but the
situations and scenes described are imaginary and although some of the
characters are based on real people their names have been changed.
In relation to those characters not based on real people any similarity to
any person living or dead is purely coincidental.

A CIP record for this book
is available from the British Library

ISBN 978-1-78148-979-6

Contents

Dedication

This book is dedicated to my long-suffering family: to my wife, Julie and my two sons, Aaron and Joshua. They have been inspirational in the content of this book and other works. It is also dedicated to the Mallorcan people of The Soller Valley, who continue to share this little piece of paradise, with ever increasing numbers of foreigners, with generosity and decorum.

Chapter 1

A Second Chance

James stared vacantly at the computer monitor, momentarily transfixed by the rhythmic pulsing of the on-screen curser, sedating him with its metronomic beat. Any pretence of waiting for inspiration, had waned several minutes earlier and all hope of 'a Eureka moment' had dissipated, in his quest to conjure up an appropriate name for his new venture; namely the small boutique hotel. He had toiled on its renovation religiously throughout the long, balmy Mallorcan summer and its opening was imminent. This was a cause of frustration for James, who felt the devil was in the details and his hotel's name was an important facet, which would require its title to be suitable and to have gravitas, as was befitting an establishment of this type.

His gaze was diverted by the shadowy movement of the outline of a nascent gecko, warming itself within the confines of an antique-style streetlight that adorned the wall of the house opposite, clearly visible from the vantage point of his first floor study window. Its closeness to the light-source, provided the voyeur with a sharp image of its profile, giving the impression that it was in fact, a painting on glass. Geckos were indigenous to the island and although he had a fondness for these unblinking little lizards, any prerequisite association between his hotel's name and geckos, simply didn't seem pertinent.

He exhaled in frustration and stood up, causing his chair to bemoan his predicament, in solidarity, with a protracted screech of its legs which vibrated on the tiled floor, akin to chalk on a blackboard. In some ways James was a perfectionist. The hotel's name, for him, was the first point of reference his prospective clientele would have. Too pretentious a name and you come across as being smug and conceited. Inappropriate, well, was just, inappropriate.

Many of the local hotels in the area had adopted the Catalan word Ca'n, meaning 'house of', followed by the name of the Mallorcan family who had once owned the building, such as Ca'n Reus or Ca'n Verdera in Fornalutx. James was not privy to the history of who had owned the derelict building he had purchased, next to his own house in Carrer de San Sebastia, that he was converting into the hotel, other than name Rodriguez on the 'escritura', or deeds, which was the surname of the couple from Valencia, from whom he had made the purchase. Ca'n Rodriguez was a bastardised vision, mixing Spanish and Catalan and James quickly dismissed it with a degree of mockery. His air of superiority was short-lived, with the realisation that his hotel was due to have its launch party in a fortnight and he still had all his marketing and branded merchandising to produce and, as yet, it was nameless.

Despite the urgency required to fix his predicament, James for the first time in a long time, realised that a degree of normality had returned to his life, since moving to his beloved Fornalutx. It had certainly been a baptism of fire for the former police detective and his family, since they moved to the village six months previously, during which time James had, unwittingly, placed the lives of his family of two young boys and his wife Charlotte, as well as his own, in grave danger.

Although life had returned to a closer vestige of normality for him since his attack, he still did not have closure. James' nemesis, Danny Kusemi, was on remand in Palma prison, awaiting trial and until he knew Kusemi was firmly behind bars, serving a life sentence, James could not totally relax. He had thrown himself into his work, in the creation of the small hotel that his wife, Charlotte and he would run. Both his sons, Adam and Reuben, seemed to be bearing no lasting mental scars of the ordeal that had befallen the family.

James was impressed by Adam, who was only eleven and who had had the stress of being bound and gagged and held against his will for over 24 hours and had later seen the aftermath of his father, having had to fight for his life, in the supposed safety of the family home. Adam, in the following weeks of the summer, seemed to have put the incidents behind him and appeared, on the surface at least, to be enjoying his new Mallorcan life.

Such events may have made most people question the logic, in remaining in a place where such brutal incidents had taken place and indeed Inspector Martinez had pointed out to James the possibility that Kusemi might still try to exact some form of retribution by proxy on him. It was something that James had considered at length, as whether his obstinacy, should be allowed to continue to keep his family in harm's way. Along with

Charlotte, they had concluded, that the sort of life that they had envisaged for themselves, but more so for their two boys, was worth the calculated risk. Risk could be assessed and steps taken for it to be reduced. This attempt at risk reduction had manifested itself, in the installation of a state of the art security system, for both James' home and for the hotel next door.

James, during his previous career as a police officer, in both London and more so in Belfast, had to be security conscious and took certain precautions regarding his movements. He was always discrete in what information he disclosed regarding his work and was generally alert to any situations that might arise, which may compromise him. Charlotte had often complained to him, that he could never fully relax, or that if he went into certain social situations, he was always pointing out the negatives. For James though, the genie was out of the bottle. Through his experience in the police, he could never look at the world again through naïve eyes. If they ever went to a concert, or event with crowds of people, he was very aware of the danger of pickpockets and in any case, he didn't like his personal space being invaded by some drunken revellers, so he tended not to want to be right at the front, or in the melee, or to throw caution to the wind and not worry about where the exits where, in case of an emergency. He couldn't help himself: he was trained that way. It was now in his DNA.

Even in more every day, mundane situations, Charlotte tended to criticize James' reaction to other people, telling him he lacked tolerance of other peoples' less well-honed skills, such as driving. James, would reply that he would excuse and be sympathetic towards genuine errors but in Mallorca, in general, he felt the standard of driving was poor and in many cases, which he came across first hand, they firmly fell into the category of careless and dangerous. Knowing your own limitations and that of your vehicle, was no more apt, than around the hazardous, narrow streets of Fornalutx and Soller, where some of the locals seemed to think it showed strength of character to continue at speed, upon meeting another car at one of the many points in the roads, which narrowed to barely a car's width. Their lack of judgement and care, they wore like a proud badge of honour on their cars, in the form of the numerous dents and marks, some of which, resembled the cratered surface of the moon. Thus, displaying their previous battle scars in a 'better get out of my way as I don't give a damn' kind of attitude.

James did not suffer fools gladly, or those who put the lives of his family or him at risk, so he inevitably felt antagonism towards people like Danny Kusemi and their ilk, who ignored the rules that are put in place by a civilised society, to keep order and to stop things from descending into chaos. He was, however, no 'job-sworth'. There were some 'rules' of the less important variety, that occasionally, necessity made for them to be broken, within the realms of minor misdemeanours. He would also contend that occasionally, in matters of graver concerns, the end justified the means. However, over recent years, as more disclosure into the murky world of 'The Troubles' in Northern Ireland had become available, he was beginning to question this mantra. Through his own first hand experiences in murder investigations that he worked on in Belfast, over a decade before, the end was sometimes hard to justify by the means used, by some of his former colleagues from a sister department: RUC Special Branch. It had made some investigations in which he was involved, in his remit as a CID Detective, almost impossible to solve.

He was not easily intimidated. He was a man of principal, albeit he had his flaws. Where he saw injustices, he simply would not walk on by. He had sacrificed a profitable business in England and a settled way of life and career path within the world of commerce, which he had embarked upon, following his decision to change his occupation to one that was more conducive to family life and for a decade, he had followed that life path. However, having glimpsed what life could be like in a new Utopia that was The Soller Valley, James was content to give all that up.

They had sold up everything they owned in the UK: their home, their business, their cars, everything. They had invested heavily, both financially and emotionally, in setting up a new life, a better life, on the island of Mallorca and specifically in Fornalutx. He was not going to sacrifice his family's chance of happiness, just because of a bitter lemon like Danny Kusemi. This was their second chance.

His thoughts returned to the task in hand and to the christening of his hotel. The Spanish word 'manana', for once, appeared to be apt and with a half-hearted attempt to suppress a yawn, he made his way to the top floor of his house, where Charlotte, his wife, was sitting on the roof terrace, armed with two of her most favoured possessions: a glass of red wine and her Kindle.

"What are you reading?" asked James.

"The Kite Runner," replied Charlotte.

"Ah yes. Well, anyway I'm going to have an early night and before you ask, no I haven't come up with a name yet, well, not one I like anyway," he said.

"Oh by the way, the hotel toiletries should be arriving from Scottish Fine Soaps tomorrow. The courier company will ring half an hour beforehand. It's just; I'm going to go for a run in the morning. Night then," he added.

The next morning, he awoke to the usual cacophony of birdsong that greeted him every morning but which was earlier and louder in the summer months, due to the early sunrise and the fact that the bedroom windows were flung wide open, in an effort to afford any vestige of anything, even half-resembling a cool summer breeze. James found the heat of a Mallorcan summer stifling. He could cope with being out in the heat of the day and anyway there was always the respite of shade, or a cooling drink, or a dip in a pool, or the nearby sea to help. Night-time was a different animal for him. He needed a good seven hours of sleep to function properly the next day; otherwise he was like a bear with a sore head without it. Charlotte could not sleep with a whirring air-conditioning unit above her head, even with ear plugs in. He felt like this was his guilty pleasure, as he yearned for the windows to be closed and the cooling wafts of machine-filtered air, to gently pass over his brow, allowing him to drift off to sleep. He had been making an effort to acclimatise to the night heat but found little succour in the allowed usage of the overhead fan. It was not uncommon for him to be seduced by the lure of the living room sofa, in order for him to get his fix of aircon but on this occasion, he had managed to drift off, without paying homage to his manmade ventilation.

He was the only one up in the house, so he quietly put on his running gear and gingerly walked about the house, searching for his iPod, without which, the necessary evil of running, would prove almost unbearable. After several minutes of inanely looking in every possible location, its repatriation proved fruitless. James vowed never again to lend it to his sons or Charlotte, not even if their lives depended on it. Wondering whether he could survive the drudgery of road-running without his music for inspiration, despite the dramatic and stunning scenery, along any route he chose to take, James, on passing the kitchen, to his delight spotted his 'precious' and quickly realised its current location, attached to the charger, had been all his own doing. His haste to blame other, completely innocent parties, might have been ill-advised, in retrospect, he thought. Happy to be reunited with his crutch, James bounded out the front door with a measure of exhilaration.

He tackled the numerous steps down to the plaça, two at a time and turned left past the bakery, heading up the hill, which would take him on a steady climb, leading out of the village to the north. There were already quite a few people embracing the new day, either opening up the cafes in the plaça for breakfast, or early delivery van drivers, bringing in fresh stock for the restaurants and the village shop.

He could see the familiar figure of Kurt, a local resident, originally from Germany, walking towards him, with his two terrier dogs, on the first of his several daily dog-walking outings.

"Hola! Buenas!" both said simultaneously, as they passed each other.

It was not unusual for him to encounter someone of another nationality, other than Mallorcan, out on his run, or in his day-to-day life. There were residents within the village, or the wider Soller Valley, from all parts of the UK and Ireland, from France, Germany, Belgium, Sweden, Australia, Romania, South Africa, Brazil, Argentina and the USA. Everyone had their own story to tell but they all had one thing in common: their appreciation of the beauty of this 'hidden Mallorca'.

He continued his ascent out of the main cluster of houses of the village, until the road now provided a bird's eye view, looking down on the tightly packed, ochre-coloured houses, which sat neatly along the ridge within the valley. The only movement came from the three flags, flapping in the breeze, on top of the castelled tower of the 'Adjuntament' or local council office building. From this position, James could marvel at the neatness of the stonework of the terracing all around the village, making use of every last piece of useable ground for lemon, orange or olive trees. The clock on the village church announced that it was now eight o'clock and beads of sweat were already forming on his head, as he persevered with the steep incline that his route provided.

A Lycra-clad cyclist freewheeled past him, heading downhill in the direction of the village. This was a far cry from earlier months and indeed was a taste of what would come later in the year, when the Valley's number would be swollen by an influx of dedicated road cycling enthusiasts, who tested themselves on the many kilometres of arduous mountain roads that the area had become so famous for, amongst the cycling fraternity.

He continued until he reached the top of the road and at that point changed to a new playlist on his iPod, which was strapped to his arm, making him look like an escaped patient from a doctor's surgery, half way through having his blood pressure taken. It was partly due to such a situation, that James had vowed to make a change to his lifestyle. Whilst living in England, he had found that his blood pressure was slightly higher than it should be and that his cholesterol levels were higher than recommended. Like a large percentage of the forty plus male population, he had been prescribed statins, to assist in reducing his cholesterol levels. Although he had always thought of himself as being reasonably fit and he still enjoyed playing sport, he had always been heavy for his height. He put this down to years of playing rugby and due to his continuation with weight training. He felt though, that this was the perfect time to get fitter than he had been for many years. His goal was to lose a stone, tone up by running twenty kilometres per week, regular weight training sessions, including cardio workouts but equally important was his desire to overhaul his diet and therefore negate the need to take statins at all. Since embarking on this six months previously, he was now half-way to achieving his goal, weight-wise and he had taken full advantage of the available bounty of locally produced fresh fruit and vegetables, no more so than the sweet Canonet orange variety, found only in the Valley.

The Soller Valley was known as Vall de Taronges in Catalan, which meant valley of the oranges and these oranges were all around him in Fornalutx. This area had the perfect climate for these oranges to thrive in. It was a special climate, slightly different from the rest of Mallorca. It also had an abundance of water in the form of torrents, streams and irrigation, first introduced by the Moors in the tenth century. Added to this was the intense moisture, the fertility of the ground and almost year round sun, creating all the necessary ingredients for the perfect orange grove. By the fifteenth century, sweet oranges had been planted in the area and were still thriving.

James headed back the way he had come, admiring the thriving fruit trees all around him on both sides of the road. He could not only see the many varieties of orange trees and lemon trees but also clementine, kiwi, avocado and pomegranate. He paused the track on his iPod momentarily, just to feel more at home with this scene of nature around him, as he continued to jog back towards the village. He stared up at the rugged, pine and olive-clad Serra de Tramuntana, the mountains which overshadowed him, towards Puig Major, its highest peak, reflecting on their sheer beauty, that never failed to impress him.

As he re-entered Fornalutx, he took a swig from his drinks bottle and continued past Plaça d'Espagne, which was noticeably busier than when he had left twenty minutes before and he continued downhill, heading in the direction of Soller. Once he had turned a corner beyond the memorial, he felt it prudent to zigzag from one side of the road to the other, in an effort to avoid being hit by oncoming vehicles, as they navigated around the tightly twisting bends. In doing so, he became aware of one of the areas many 'characters' in the middle distance. A short distance in front of him, making his daily pilgrimage to Fornalutx from his home in the neighbouring hamlet of Biniaraix, was a man, who James and his boys called 'The Hippy Shepherd'. He was a man in his late sixties, with long, straggly grey hair and a beard, sporting a baseball hat, which looked somewhat foreign on the head of a man of his years. He was wearing a brightly-coloured, short-sleeved, Hawaiian shirt, which was unbuttoned, revealing quite a tanned but sizeable gut. He was bedecked with a pair of walking boots and a pair of cargo shorts, whilst carrying not such an inconsequential shepherd's crook to assist in his amble. James nodded in recognition from behind his sunglasses as he passed and plodded onwards towards his destination, namely the local football stadium in Soller. This was where he turned to come back to Fornalutx, giving him a more than ample five kilometres of a run, which he had been doing four times a week for the last three months. He would deviate from the normal route occasionally, by driving the short distance to the Port de Soller and run between the two lighthouses and back, giving him a change of scenery of a similar distance.

As he returned to the plaça, he paused at the bottom of the steps, switched off his iPod, dried the sweat on his face with his top and gulped down the last remaining few mouthfuls of water from his drinks bottle. He stood with his hands on his knees, visibly panting from his exertion, when from behind him, he heard a familiar voice with a hint of Afrikaans say;

"Oh I do like a man in Lycra!"

James turned to see the jovial South African Paul approach him, in company with his dog Brandy.

"I haven't seen you for a while. Shouldn't you be turning down some beds or cooking breakfast or something, instead of galavanting all around the village, getting sweaty in tight shorts?" asked Paul, with a rueful grin.

"Well, I'll be doing just that in a little over a week. That is, if I can ever come up with a name for the damn place!" replied James.

"Why don't you call it Moulin Noir or something exotic?" asked Paul.

"That sounds like a tart's boudoir!" laughed James. "I still can't decide and I've so much still to get printed. It's a nightmare but we'll get there. Are you coming to the opening?"

"Of course. I wouldn't miss it for the world. By the way, we missed you in the square on Friday evening for drinks. Your good lady was there," said Paul.

"Yeah, sorry. Ulster were playing a pre-season game of rugby against Munster, which I didn't want to miss. There are a couple of your guys who play for Ulster," started James.

"What, gay guys?" asked Paul, with an inquisitive look.

"No, I meant South Africans. Anyway, it was an incredible game and I couldn't get away. Ulster were 10 points down with 10 minutes to go but the Ulster guys put in some massive tackles. They had to come from behind but they scored two tries in the last five minutes to win," said James.

"I love rugby. I think maybe it's just because I like men in tight shorts. Anyway! Talking of massive tackles, I've got to go and see my little friend," said Paul, turning in the direction of home with a wave.

"See you later", called James after him.

"Bye darling, bye!" he called back, drawing a smile from James.

James sauntered up the steps of the plaça to his street, pausing briefly to allow the completion of a photo opportunity by a couple of tourists. The urge to 'photobomb' the composition was great but he controlled his urge and strolled the remaining few steps to his house. Opening the door into the entrada, he noted that there was a package on the dining table. He attempted to open the package but he realised that it had been triple-wrapped in some sort of anti-nuclear titanium strength shrink-wrap and he surmised that any future exertion would be pure folly, so instead, he made a beeline for his industrial strength Stanley knife, which made short shrift of the Krypton Factor test. After removing a full morning's output of a Chinese factory's polystyrene, he found the hidden prize within; namely his new promotional brochures for his hotel.

In a scene reminiscent of a child opening presents on Christmas morning, James, on finding his brochure, produced a broad grin of pride, mixed with anxiety, at the thought of the hard work it was going to take to fill the place with satisfied and hopefully returning guests. He scanned through the glossy brochure, admiring the photography but at the same time, reading the content for any mistakes, despite having checked and re-checked the copy, before printing approval had been given. All he needed now was to have a suitable hotel name emblazoned on the front.

'Not bad at all,' he concluded, on completion.

If anything, seeing his transformation from a derelict wreck to quite a stylish and apparently photogenic building, gave him a sense of optimism, that filling his new hotel may not be as arduous a task as he first thought. Buoyed by his new found confidence and enthusiastic to show the brochure to Charlotte, he found some extra energy and tackled the steep stairs two at a time, whilst calling to her to inform her of his discovery. Charlotte had obviously signed for the package and was aware of its arrival and although not wanting to completely dampen his enthusiasm, she received the brochure with mock excitement and reverence.

"Alright, alright!" protested James, with an air of indignation. "It may not be a big thing for you but it is for me. Have a look and tell me what you think."

She flicked through the brochure, before tacitly nodding her head. James' face bore an ever-growing smile, before he said enthusiastically,

"Now, that's the sort of place where I would want to stay!"

"I have to admit the photos came out really well. I'm glad we got Sean to do them. Not bad at all," said Charlotte, returning the brochure to an exuberant James.

"Not bad!" exclaimed James, "It's like something out of a Homes and Interiors magazine!"

"Even your cushions look good," retorted Charlotte, in a jibe to James, over his obsession with getting the interior just right, even down to the cushions.

"If that's a compliment, I'll take it. What about the extra crockery and glasses? I think I'll just get them from Ikea. I need a trip to Palma anyway, so I think I'll go there this afternoon. There's nothing like some retail therapy and I need to pick up a couple of my order items from Zara Home," said James, as he climbed the stairs, heading for the shower.

A short time later, he set off for Palma in order to get some extra items for the hotel opening and for some finishing touches to the hotel guest rooms. His first port of call was the large IKEA store on the fringes of Palma. It was a pleasant trip for James, who didn't mind shopping trips for kitchenware or interior items, no matter how mundane the items were. He quite enjoyed walking round IKEA, gleaning ideas from their various room sets but he usually made do with the odd accessory or fabric. He felt that their best products were in the kitchen department, as having previously owned a furniture business; he couldn't bring himself to put flat-pack furniture either in his home or his hotel.

He filled a trolley with additional crockery and several sizes of wine glasses and hi-ball glasses and made his way to the checkout. As he did so, he stood behind a couple at the checkout. The man turned to the side and James instantly recognised him as being a former childhood hero of his, Gerry Armstrong. He recalled the former Northern Ireland footballer's winning goal against Spain in the 1982 Football World Cup. Gerry, he remembered, had later signed for Real Mallorca and still commentated on Spanish football games for UK television. Feeling a little bold, James initiated a conversation, slightly intensifying his mild Northern Irish accent,

"Ach, what about ye Gerry?"

Gerry turned around and instantaneously held out his hand, graciously, as if he was meeting an old friend,

"Ach, how are you doin'? What are you at, yourself?" he enquired.

"Oh, I'm just getting a few extra things for our hotel opening in Fornalutx. I know you live here on the island but whereabouts are you based?" asked James.

"We're down near Santa Ponsa and we are just putting in a new kitchen," added Gerry.

The two men chatted like two old friends and James bid his former hero goodbye when he had finished packing his goods. He wondered whether he should have invited Gerry to the hotel opening but then remembered Gerry had told him he was commentating for SKY TV around the date of the opening.

James continued into Palma and made his way to Porto Pi, a shopping centre at the eastern end of the city. The shopping centre was busy and he had to contend with several 'moving walkways', to get to the appropriate level where Zara Home was. The moving walkways were slow moving and he found himself becoming impatient with the numerous other people in front of him, who were casually standing and allowing themselves to be transported along at a snail's pace. 'That would have been fine and their prerogative, if only they weren't blocking the already narrow walkway,' he thought. James bit his tongue for the whole of the first one but on descending down another level, he could not contain himself any longer, thinking to himself, 'These are called moving WALKWAYS for a reason, people!'

In a slightly raised voice, which appeared to scare a couple immediately in front of him, James managed to complete his journey in record time saying,

"Pasando! Perdona!" as he passed.

He couldn't blame the apathy on the 'manana' temperament of the Spanish, as he noted English and German being spoken by some of the people as he passed them. He knew what Charlotte would have said, "Tranquillo! Just relax and slow it down a bit".

He had things to do and although he didn't run around like a headless chicken, he nonetheless, preferred to operate in efficient mode. He arrived at his destination and picked up some table lights he had ordered and noticed a couple of what Charlotte referred to as 'non-essential items' but he knew they would look good in the guest bedrooms and unable to resist, made the additional purchases. 'These are business expenses and are tax deductible,' he assured himself, as he headed back to the car, armed with several shopping bags. Not wishing to bash people with his bags, he allowed himself to be returned to his parking level, once again, via the moving walkways, but this time he went with the flow and kept his temperament in check.

On his return to Fornalutx, James carried his various purchases into the hotel in a covert manner, so as not to have proceedings instigated against him, similar to those suffered during The Spanish Inquisition. He was in no doubt that he would have been subjected to such, if Charlotte had discovered his additional 'unnecessary purchases'. Having found new homes for his 'accessories' and pleased with their addition to the overall scheme of the hotel, he returned home.

Chapter 2

The Grand Opening

"Have we got enough canapés? Did you get those extra bottles of cava I asked for?" demanded an agitated James of Charlotte, as he walked to and fro in the entrada of the hotel.

As he did so, he made a minor adjustment to the position of some trays of nibbles on a table, fully laden with countless offerings of food. The table legs appeared to be straining under the sheer weight of a huge array of alcoholic beverages.

"Would you calm down!" exclaimed Charlotte. "Stop stressing out. It's not the feeding of the five thousand. You've put far too much out. How many people do you think are coming, for goodness sake? Look, go and have a stiff drink or something. This is only a party for some friends to show them how the place looks," said Charlotte, in an exasperated tone.

"Plus the mayor and the photographers and Soller Sheila is doing an article for *The Majorcan Daily Bulletin* and various others. Anyway, I just want everything to be as good as it can be. I've put a lot of work into this place and I just want tonight to run smoothly. You're right though; I do need to calm down a bit. Maybe a gin and tonic is a good idea," retorted James.

He broke the seal and unscrewed the cap off a bottle of Hendrick's Gin, poured himself a generous measure and added ice and lemon before adding the tonic, causing the glass to fill to almost overflowing, in a cascade of effervescence. James took a large gulp from the glass, getting an instant hit of tangy juniper berry and lemon. Feeling instantly refreshed and slightly calmer, he went back for a second mouthful, taking in a quickly diminishing ice cube, and in so doing, allowed himself the pleasure of crunching the cube between his teeth, cooling his mouth in the process.

He opened the front door of the hotel and walked a few paces away, turned and looked back at the façade. He couldn't help but beam with pride at the finished article but was especially impressed with the new, locally designed and crafted hanging sign with subtle backlighting, announcing to all and sundry, that Hotel Artesa was open for business. James considered himself to be a creative person and he took an interest in local architecture, customs and art. In his deliberations on a name for the hotel, he thought of a way to decorate the hotel in a stylish manner that would also celebrate some of the local artists, crafts people and artisans, by displaying their creations in both the guest bedrooms and the communal areas of the hotel. In keeping with this promotion of local culture, the name Hotel Artesa, meaning Hotel Artisan, was born.

He was very pleased with the array of art that he was displaying. There were muted watercolours depicting local scenes, sculptures in bronze and terracotta, vibrantly-coloured and framed batik scarves and original black and white framed photographs, showing some of the local people and places during the 1950s and 1960s, giving the cool white walls a deliberate retro, almost gallery style. The artwork would be changed from time to time and would be for sale to guests, thus showcasing local talent and allowing the hotel to metamorphosize.

He returned inside, upon hearing chatter and laughter getting closer, coming from the direction of the plaça. Assuming these were the first of his guests for the opening, he wanted one last check on operations inside. Satisfied that everything was fine, he turned to Charlotte, clicked his heels together Gestapo-style, played with an imaginary monocle at one eye and glaring at her, asked in the best German accent he could muster:

"Alles in ordnung?"

Charlotte simply shook her head and tutted, not overly impressed by James' attempt at parodying himself.

Sure enough, moments later, a group of Charlotte and James' friends and residents of Soller arrived, as did many more. He had invited the mayor to attend, to cut a ribbon to mark the official opening of the newest addition to the Fornalutx, small but exclusive hotel set. After about half an hour of mingling with friends and local dignitaries, James had managed to greet everyone and talk to about a dozen of the forty plus ensemble. The hotel entrada was full to capacity, with several guests spilling onto the pedestrianised cobbled street to the front. It was here that James caught the eye of his friend Matt, who had attended with Jayne, his wife. James and Matt had been good friends during the years that he and his family had been holidaying in Fornalutx and he had assisted at the exchange of his son, Adam, in returning the stolen money James had recovered belonging to Kusemi. However, over the preceding couple of months, Matt had been surprisingly aloof.

James had been extremely busy in getting the hotel renovated, during a time when most builders shut down for their holidays, as he felt it was good therapy to throw himself into his work and finances dictated an early start date would be necessary, to get as many of the remaining visitors of the season to stay in Hotel Artesa.

He had spoken to Matt briefly, after Kusemi had been charged and remanded to Palma prison awaiting trial and things on that occasion seemed fine. It was only after James' vivid dream, that he concluded that Matt could have had the opportunity and maybe even the motive, to have had some part to play in the murder of Chas Daly, the body of whom James had found. No matter how ridiculous it seemed and the fact that there was absolutely no evidence linking Matt Smith, his friend, to a vicious murder, literally two streets from where they now stood, James' gut told him that something was not right and that Matt knew more than he was letting on.

He went outside, to greet Matt and Jayne.

"Hey! Lovely to see you both. Thanks for coming," he started, shaking Matt's hand and kissing Jayne. "I haven't seen you for ages. How long has it been?" asked James.

"It's been over a month," replied Jayne. "I thought you two had fallen out or something, because we hadn't seen or heard from you for so long. I said to grumpy drawers here, why don't you call James or go and see him? He will need a friend right now and you know what he said, James?" asked Jayne.

"No, what?" replied James.

"Give the guy some space. He's been through a lot. If he needs me, he'll call, so just to let you know, I have been thinking about you but I know you've been incredibly busy. This place looks amazing!" she said, walking into the entrada, leaving James, now alone outside with Matt.

"How have you been?" asked Matt, in a subdued voice.

"Fine, mate, fine. I've been very busy, otherwise I would have called… you know…" started James.

"Yeah, yeah," interrupted Matt. "Listen, I should have called round, even after that day I saw you, after, you know…" continued Matt, stumbling awkwardly over his words.

A momentary awkward silence was broken by James, when he said;

"Well then… shall I give you the grand tour?"

"Of course, but listen, you see to your other guests. I'll grab a drink and catch you later," said Matt, motioning with his hands for James to go to his other guests, while heading towards the drinks table.

Just as James turned to speak to other guests, he turned his head back in Matt's direction, as Matt added; "Oh and James… we need to talk but not tonight. Tonight's your night".

His words completely caught James off guard. He wanted to find out what he had to say and his imagination was now running away with him. He was now in the company of other friends and he could see their lips moving as they talked to him and smiled but all he could concentrate on was what Matt had said. James felt it similar to a situation, when someone might say; "I've a bone to pick with you but I can't stop now", and you're left to wonder what on earth it could be that you have said or done and it usually isn't because they want to thank you for something. Could James' theory about Matt be right? Did he have something to get off his chest? He was itching to get Matt in private and find out why exactly he felt they needed to talk.

"James? Did you James?"

"Sorry. What was that Sarah?" asked James of his friend, who had clearly been asking him something but his mind was elsewhere.

"I just wanted to know if you got Xavi Mayol to do those terracotta sculptures specifically for here or had he already done them?" asked a slightly annoyed Sarah, realising that James had not been giving her his complete attention.

"Sorry Sarah. It's not you. It has been a long haul on very little sleep and these gin and tonics are pretty strong. No, he made them specifically for the three spaces there," replied James, with an apologetic tone.

His reply appeared to lift Sarah but just then, James noticed a man, whom he did not recognise or recall having greeted at the front door. He appeared to be by himself and he was standing with his back to James, about twenty feet away, staring at some of the framed photographs on the far wall of the entrada.

"Excuse me, would you?" said James and he made his way towards the man. He came alongside the man, who was tall and of athletic build. He glanced up at the stranger, who was about forty years of age, with thick, dark, well-groomed hair and he was wearing a dark linen suit and a low-necked T-shirt, revealing a well-defined, muscular torso.

"Have you seen any of Tom Weedon's work before?" asked James, in an effort to strike up a conversation with the stranger.

"I have not," replied the man succinctly and with what James took to be a Russian accent.

"He certainly caught the feeling of a bygone era. I'm James Gordon, owner of Hotel Artesa," said James, extending his hand to the man, who continued to look straight ahead at the photographs.

"They say the eyes are the windows to the soul, do they not? I know who you are Mr Gordon. I am here simply to pass on a message from a client. I was not sure whether it is the correct practice at such events to bring a present, but I brought one for you anyway," said the stranger, who reached into his jacket pocket and produced a small, gift-wrapped box, about the size of a matchbox. It was only when the man presented it to him, that he noticed that he was wearing black leather gloves.

James' heart began to beat faster and he felt uncomfortable by the actions of this man. He was looking directly at the man now but he was still not looking James in the eye. He was about to return his outstretched hand to his side, as there was clearly not going to be a handshake but before he could, the man had placed the small box in his hand.

"Sorry, who are you?" asked James quickly. "What do you mean a message from a client? Which client?" he added.

The man suddenly turned and walked assertively towards the door.

"Stop that man!" shouted James, from across the crowded room.

Everyone turned in his direction; some thinking it was perhaps part of the evening's entertainment and clapped. James thought about fighting his way past his guests and attempting to detain the stranger but in the time it took him to ponder what to do, the man had disappeared out the door. His attention was drawn back to the object he was now holding.

Charlotte rushed over to where he was now frozen to the spot, holding the small, gift-wrapped box in the palm of his outstretched hand.

"What's happened? Who was that?" she demanded.

Before he could answer, Matt had joined them.

"What's happened?" said a concerned Matt. "Do you want me to go after him?" he continued.

"No, leave him. I'm more concerned with this," said James, nodding towards the box.

"Should I be concerned? Should I get everyone to leave?" asked Charlotte, looking round at her guests saying, "It's alright, it's alright!"

"Stay here!" demanded James of Charlotte and Matt.

James turned and walked briskly up the stairs to the first floor and to the first guest bedroom he came to and opened the door, allowing it to close behind him. He was, by now, convinced that the stranger's 'client', was no other than Danny Kusemi and that inside the small box was some kind of 'message' designed to intimidate him, not necessarily to harm him but he didn't want to take any chances. He set the small box down on a writing table in the room. He had pretty much ruled out the miniscule box containing any sort of explosive device, due to its lack of any real weight. He estimated that it may only be around five to ten grammes, in total. If he called the police, they may require him to evacuate the hotel of all his guests, as a precautionary measure, which would be sure to put a dampener on the whole opening and may bring the completely wrong type of publicity for the hotel, which he could ill afford. Conscious of potential forensic evidence but realising that it was extremely unlikely; James carefully opened the wrapping paper, to reveal a matchbox. He had seen some incendiary devices that had been about this size, but concluded that he would not have simply been handed something, which he could quite easily dispose of, before any intended damage could be caused.

He carefully but nervously pushed the forefinger of his right hand into the inner part of the matchbox, revealing a piece of cotton wool inside. From the weight, James knew there was something else inside. He lifted the small piece of cotton wool up, to reveal what he had suspected he might find. Staring back at him was a 9mm calibre parabellum bullet. He knew this was the most popular and widespread handgun bullet in the world. He had used similar .38 special rounds himself, as his personal protection weapon, as a serving police officer, had been a Ruger speed six revolver.

He had expected that something like this might happen. He had just not expected it at the most inconvenient time possible. He lifted the box containing the bullet and secreted it in the drawer of the writing desk in the guest room, resolved to not let it spoil his event. He would inform Inspector Martinez the moment the last invited guest had departed. He was also conscious of the fact that images of the unwanted guest, should have been caught on his new CCTV system, which was in operation.

James returned to the entrada and assured Charlotte and Matt that any impending disaster was not going to happen and continued with the event, showing his guests all six of the sumptuously decorated guest rooms and the little courtyard to the rear. After posing for numerous photographs and giving sufficient information to allow Soller Sheila, a local expat resident and journalist, to promote the hotel on her website and for a piece in the main English language newspaper on the island, James thanked the last remaining guests for their attendance and closed and locked the doors. Matt had asked to stay and help but James had not wanted to involve him further, especially in light of what he had said. He felt he had had enough excitement for one night and any revelations from him could wait until the following day.

He had the personal mobile number of Inspector Ramon Martinez, which he rang.

"Hola! Dime," came the recognisable voice of Inspector Martinez.

"Ramon. It's me," said James.

"Hey, James. How did the opening go? I'm sorry I couldn't be there, as I had to work tonight but I appreciated your invitation. What can I do for you?"

"I've just had a visit from a friend of Kusemi. It had to be tonight of all nights!" exclaimed James.

"Tell me what's happened," said a concerned Martinez.

"I noticed someone at the opening tonight who I didn't recognise and I went over to speak to him.

He said he knew who I was and that he was there to give me a message from a client or something and he then handed me a small gift-wrapped box. Before I could do anything about it, he had left. To cut a long story short, I've been sent a bullet: that's my message. This guy looked like a pro, ex-military, a hitman. He spoke English but with a strong, what I think was, a Russian accent. I am going to check the CCTV but hopefully he will be on it. Look, can your coming over here, wait until the morning? I've secured the bullet in the box. I doubt if there will be much gleaned by forensics, as he wore gloves. Look, I'll check the CCTV and I can see you in the morning, if that suits," continued James.

"OK, James. We'll not lose anything by waiting until tomorrow. I can call with you at the hotel at say, 10 o'clock, mas o menos. OK?" asked Martinez.

"That's fine, Ramon. We said something like this was bound to happen but it still doesn't make it any easier. Hasta luego," said James.

"Hasta manana. Adios".

He checked the CCTV footage of the evening, while Charlotte returned next door to their adjoining house, having checked on their boys and the babysitter every fifteen minutes after the incident that evening. There was clear footage of the man from behind but no clear footage from the front but he thought that perhaps the images could be enhanced to such an extent, as to put a name to the face. James secured the disk and retrieved the box and bullet from the first floor and placed them in the hotel safe. He couldn't do any more that evening, except to try and convince Charlotte that their decision to stay, despite the risks, had been the right one. It was going to be a long night.

Chapter 3

A Cold Front from the East

A loud blast of 'I'm Shipping up to Boston' by The Dropkick Murphys, came from the direction of the adjacent kitchen worktop, alerting James to the fact that he had an incoming call on his mobile phone. With his head drooped over his breakfast bowl of Weetabix and blueberries, the unwelcome din had awakened him from his slumber and he rushed to answer the call, before his ringtone reached its pinnacle in rowdiness, in case it wakened, if it hadn't already, a still sleeping Charlotte.

It had been a fairly sleepless night for James, who had spent the first couple of hours attempting to appease Charlotte and to reassure her, that despite this latest setback, things in their Garden of Eden, were still rosy. The fact that, in gardening terms, someone kept spraying their 'garden' with copious amounts of DDT, making replanting in ever-increasingly toxic soil almost impossible, didn't help. He felt that exhaustion over the subject matter, rather than a successful resolution to their problem, had been the reason they had stopped the debate and finally got some staccato sleep. The last thing he wanted to do was wake Charlotte at this early hour. Having been unable to get into his usual, deep, fully snoring sleep, he had got up to reassess their predicament.

He grabbed his mobile and saw that it was a call from Ramon.

"Hola, Ramon," he answered.

"Hola, James. I am sorry to call you so early but I thought you might be up. I need to see the CCTV footage from last night and to take the bullet for examination, first thing, as there was a serious incident in Sa Pobla overnight that demands my attention and I don't know how long I will be there for, so I will be at your hotel in twenty minutes. OK?" asked Inspector Martinez.

"Yeah, that's fine," said James, trying to find just the right volume between audible and a whisper.

James finished his breakfast and made his way next door to his hotel and opened up. He went to the safe behind the reception desk in the entrada and recovered the CCTV recording and the bullet still retained in its box, in anticipation of the arrival of Martinez. He did not have long to wait, as a few minutes later, in walked an ebullient Inspector Martinez, with a discernible smile on his face.

"I'm glad to see someone at least has something to smile about," said James, setting both items of evidence on the reception desk for him to see.

"Sorry. It's just, two minutes ago I was told that I no longer have to go to Sa Pobla after all. For me, that is definitely a reason to be happy. I will let you into a little secret James, as the operation has now finished. A few hours ago, the night shift Inspector was asked to do a raid on an address in Sa Pobla, simultaneously with another raid in Cadiz. We had received information that an ISIS suspect was at one of two possible addresses. This morning, I was told that a man fitting the suspects' description had been detained and I was to go to the scene to co-ordinate follow up searches. I didn't want to get involved, as I reckon I would still be there tomorrow. Anyway, the good news is that the real suspect has been identified and arrested in Cadiz and the other guy in Sa Pobla is a Moroccan, who was unlucky enough to have a very similar name and description to our man. So, he has been released and I am no longer required. Good news for me but not so good for you," said Ramon, visibly frowning, in deference to James' predicament.

"You can say that again!" exclaimed James. "I got about two hours sleep last night, after trying to talk Charlotte down from twenty thousand feet. For a while, she was adamant she was leaving with the boys this morning and to be honest I don't blame her! The problem is I can't just up and leave. For a start, all our money is tied up in this place and I was really looking forward to getting this venture off the ground. I think it could really work," started James.

"I have to say, James, you have done a really good job here," interrupted Ramon, scanning the entrada and peering into the rear courtyard. "I agree with you," he continued. "If the rooms are like this, I think you will fill this place."

"Well, for what it's worth, here is my little present and the CCTV footage of Santa Claus," said James, sarcastically.

"Can I see it now?" asked Ramon.

"Sure," said James, accepting the disk back from Ramon, which he loaded into the DVD player.

He showed Ramon the whole footage of the suspect from the previous night and paused it at the point showing the suspect's face.

"That's the best shot. It's not great but perhaps the image can be enhanced," said James, retrieving the disk and returning it to Ramon.

"We will do our best James. Someone may know him just from that. I will call at the bank on the corner, in case their CCTV has got a clearer image of him, if he went passed there of course," concluded Ramon.

"Thanks for your help. I doubt you will get anything from the bullet, but let me know if there are any developments and I'll keep in touch," said James, shaking Ramon by the hand.

Ramon kept a tight grip of James' hand and said, "I think the correct English saying is 'don't let the bastards get you down'. Is that how it goes?"

"That's pretty much it, bang on," retorted James, impressed by Martinez's grasp of English expressions.

"You, Charlotte and the boys, you are Mallorcan now, eh? Maybe you are not like the Mayols or Busquets or other families who have been here for centuries but hey, you feel this is your home... I can tell. So I say to you: do not let some filthy English pig drive you and your family away or his Russian, you think, Russian servant send you away. I know you are a fighter James and I will help you in that fight. OK, amigo?" said Ramon.

"OK, sure Ramon," replied James, feeling the need to divert his gaze to the ground and avert Martinez's eye, as he suddenly became quite emotional at the speech he had just heard and was quite touched by.

"Adios!" said Martinez with a wave, as he let himself out.

James took a moment to compose himself. He was touched by the clear solidarity a fellow law enforcement officer had shown him and from someone who could see James' passion for the island and his desire to live and to try to integrate, or the closest thing to integration a non-Mallorcan could achieve. Perhaps it was the stress of the incident the previous evening and the anxiety of knowing that Charlotte was reliving the incidents of the previous six months again, coupled with sleep deprivation. Whatever the reason, James was taken aback by his own emotions.

This was quickly halted by another blast of 'I'm Shipping up to Boston' and he answered his mobile. It was Matt.

"Yes mate. How are things?" said James.

"I just wanted to check everything was fine after last night," said Matt.

"Yeah. Nothing else happened after you left. Ramon has just been here, so we will wait and see if his men can identify the guy from last night but we have to keep going," said James, trying to be positive.

"Good, good," replied Matt. "Anyway, look I need to speak to you," he added.

"Right. OK. Look, I'm here by myself at the hotel. Do you want to pop round?" asked James.

"Alright. I'll see you shortly," said Matt.

"See you then. Bye."

James hung up and put his mobile on the desk. 'What did Matt want to tell him?' he thought. He was intrigued.

His mind was coming up with numerous answers but all of them were derivations on the same theme; namely, what happened to Daly? He began pacing up and down the entrada, waiting for Matt to arrive.

Half an hour later, there was a knock on the glass door of the hotel and James looked immediately towards the door, to see Matt looking back at him.

"It's open!" he shouted towards Matt.

Matt opened the door, closing it behind him and walked the few steps into the entrada to where an expectant James was waiting.

"Can we sit down?" asked Matt, catching James' gaze but immediately looking to the floor.

"Sure. Take a seat," he said, ushering Matt to a seating area near the reception desk.

Both men sat down. A long, uncomfortable pause was broken by Matt exhaling loudly and then looking directly at James, he said;

"What I am about to tell you is very difficult for me and I want you to let me tell you the whole thing, without interruption. It might be difficult to listen to but I implore you to let me finish and then you can ask questions. Deal?" asked Matt, who was visibly shaking.

"OK. Deal," replied James, completely attentive as to what Matt was now saying.

"I haven't been completely honest with you about the whole Daly incident," began Matt, before pausing, as if he expected James to immediately start asking questions. When none came, he continued;

"The night in the plaça, when we were drinking with him, what I didn't tell you is that he was going to invest, or at least lend me €50,000 to keep my business afloat, because I'm sure you have gathered that since the recession, work has slowed up somewhat. Anyway, we were going to finalise things that night and he was going to let me have the cash the following day. When he didn't come back to the table, I was a little concerned that perhaps he had got cold feet, so when I left you, I decided to call at his house. I stopped to have a pee in the alley near his house and just as I was finishing, I saw a man coming out of his house. Now, let me tell you, I thought I had seen a ghost, because even though I hadn't seen this guy since he was about 14 years old and even though the street wasn't exactly well-lit, he looked at me and I looked at him and I recognised him, albeit he was bigger and older. I knew straight away that I had just seen Danny Kusemi. He looked at me but I knew he didn't recognise me. Well, that's because I look completely different to the 14-year-old who knew him from Salter Road Care Home in Rotherhithe."

"You were in a care home with Danny Kusemi?" James blurted out, unable to contain himself.

"James!" said Matt sternly; "We agreed no interruptions and no questions until the end."

Matt paused, looking at James, who motioned with his hand for him to continue.

"I was born in Bermondsey in 1970. I won't go into my family history other than to say, I'm sure you have heard of the Richardsons?"

Matt looked to James, who nodded in affirmation.

He continued, "Well, my birth name was Matthew Richardson. To cut a long story short, when my old man and his cronies went inside, I was very young. It was when I knew he was getting out, that I went mad and started getting into trouble. My mother didn't really love me. She was always off her tits on booze or drugs and so, I was put into care by Social Services, which is where I met Danny Kusemi. Danny and I were like brothers. I looked out for him. Other kids were scared of me because of my old man but it was a care-worker who was the problem. He started abusing Danny, sexually. Danny didn't tell me for ages, because he was too embarrassed, but when he did I went berserk and I kicked the shit out of that guy. Anyway... needless to say, I ended up in Feltham Young Offenders Institution for over a year for GBH. It was my wake-up call. It was the best thing that could have happened to me. I swore that I would not go back to Bermondsey, to my criminal family. I was going to make sure that the boy who had got himself put inside, would come out a very different young man. That kid wasn't the real me. He was a product of his surroundings and of those around him. Whilst I was in Feltham, I was visited by a Christian, who was a lecturer at Durham University. He saw the potential in me and on my release, both Charles, who I call Dad and Mabel, who I call Mum, fostered me and put me on the straight and narrow. I took their surname, Smith and I went to a good school from 15 years of age, passed my 'O' levels and 'A' levels and ended up doing a Humanities Degree at Durham University."

"Does Jayne know any of this?" interjected James.

"I'm coming to that now. No she doesn't and I don't want her to. Jayne and I met at Durham and as far as she knows, I went into foster care and that I don't know who my real parents were. She knows nothing about the Richardsons or Feltham and that's how I would like to keep it. Getting back to that night, Kusemi went out of sight and I went into Daly's house. The place was a mess and he was lying on his back, choking on his own blood. He was in a bad way but he was conscious.

"I leant down over him and he said something garbled about a key and a locker and loads of cash. He said; "Your mate has it. Your mate has it." I didn't initially know what he meant but then it dawned on me, that the key for all the cash he was talking about must be in the fag packet, which you had. It is at this point, that I did something that I am not proud of. The thought of my financial worries and the future of my kids being secure just took over and I lifted a cushion from the floor. I thought if this guy Daly is an associate of Danny Kusemi's, he doesn't deserve to have this sort of money and it has to be the proceeds of crime. I had been following Danny's career from a distance, so I knew the sort of guy he had become. Daly wasn't putting up much of a struggle but before I knew it, I could hear my father's voice in my head, I mean Charles, who had given me a Christian upbringing, and I stopped immediately. Daly was still breathing. I tell you he was still alive. He was not in a good way but he was still alive. I came to my senses and I dialled 112 for an ambulance from my mobile. To be honest, my battery was low and the signal was poor but I thought they got the address. I took out my sim card when I left the house and put it in a nearby bin. It was a pay as you go mobile but I didn't know if it could be traced to me or not.

"Now I realise that the call may have been received but the address was not clear which, I presume, is why no ambulance came. I have been living with this guilt for several months. I couldn't believe it when I heard he was dead. Whether what I did killed him, or whether it was the beating Danny gave him, is immaterial. I feel responsible for his death. So what do we do now?" asked Matt, looking up at James.

"Whoa! Give me a minute to take all this in," said James, standing up and putting his hands on his head. "To be honest, I had my suspicions that you had some part to play. I had quite a vivid dream, after Kusemi had been arrested. The fact that you knew him and are from Bermondsey... and a Richardson... well I wasn't expecting that, I can tell you," said James, shaking his head in disbelief.

"I may have had the misfortune of being born into that family but I can assure you I am not a Richardson," said Matt, obviously hurt by what his friend had just said.

"So how did Daly end up moving to Fornalutx and did you know him previously?" James asked.

"His move to Fornalutx, as far as I know, was purely random. I knew he was from Bermondsey but I never knew him, growing up. And I wasn't exactly going to tell him who I really was. His connection with Danny and me seeing Danny was just a massive coincidence. What is it they call it: six degrees of separation or something?" replied Matt.

"OK, OK. Let me think about this. Right, so you are assuring me that he was still alive when you left him and that you attempted, at least, to call an ambulance?"

"Yes. Yes, I am," pleaded Matt.

"OK, well the phone call can be checked for that night, to see if any calls were received without any speech or a broken message. I need to have that checked discretely, to see if that's true. If that's the case, well I'm not necessarily going to start telling Martinez or Jayne or anyone else about you involvement or about your past. But hang on a minute, where's the money?" asked James, remembering this crucial detail.

Before Matt could answer, James added;

"I'm just putting this together now. You nearly got me killed!" said a now animated James.

"Let me explain! Let me explain!" shouted Matt, putting his hands up in a defensive manner.

"I took most of the money out of the bag just before the handover. I replaced it with cut up newspaper but still put £100,000 of cash on the top. I thought Danny would be arrested. I had no idea that he would escape and come after you. If I had known that, I would never have taken the money," said Matt, sincerely.

"But what were you going to say had happened to the money, if he was arrested, as you expected him to be?" said James, aggressively.

"I was going to call you and ask you not to say that any money was missing; to plead my case with you because of the trouble I was in with my business. If it hadn't been for Kusemi showing up, I would have been fine. I would have got the €50k that Daly had promised me but that didn't happen. I had to think of my kids, of Jayne and I can assure you, if I had any idea that the Police would botch their job, I would never have done it."

James paced the floor, deep in thought, before turning to Matt and saying,

"So where is the money now?"

"It's hidden at my flat. I've taken a little, just to keep our heads above water but apart from the £100k that I gave to Danny at the handover, it's all there," said an anxious Matt, wondering what James was going to do.

"Here's another thing matey. You took a bag with only a portion of Danny Kusemi's money in it, knowing full well what sort of a bloke he was and knowing that if he discovered he was being screwed, that he could quite happily have done something to Adam, my son, you stupid bastard!" screamed James at Matt, whilst grabbing him round the throat and raising his fist, as if to punch him.

"James, please," sobbed Matt, as he wriggled free from his grip, "I knew Danny would never hurt Adam. He may have become a violent man but he would not hurt a defenceless boy. He's a father himself. I'm sorry if you think I risked him hurting Adam but I knew he couldn't do it, no matter what he said to you."

"Leave me a minute. Go into the courtyard there," ordered James, "I can't look at you."

Matt obliged and timidly started to make his way to the inner courtyard of the hotel, before turning to James and adding,

"Please James, let me…"

"Just go! I need to think!" barked James, pointing swiftly to the courtyard in an aggressive manner.

Matt turned and walked into the courtyard, closing the doors behind him. James walked over to the reception desk and from a drawer, retrieved a packet of cigarettes he had stashed and went outside to the front of the hotel and lit one. He was within a few feet of his own front door and was in danger of Charlotte seeing him smoking, which he knew would annoy her, but he needed something to calm him down and right at that moment, a cigarette was what he needed.

He drew quickly but firmly on the cigarette, so much so, that he felt a little light-headed.

'Oh what a bloody mess!' he thought, as he paced up and down a few steps from the door, whilst peering through to the courtyard, to make sure Matt was still there. 'It would have been no mean feat for him to scale the 20 foot walls of the courtyard', he thought. He hurriedly finished the cigarette, tossing the butt on the cobbled street and put it out with his heel, whilst having the forethought to collect the evidence and discard it in the hotel bin inside. Still not having concluded what his next move would be, he made his way back to the courtyard doors and beckoned Matt back inside, in case their conversation could have been overheard by Charlotte, next door.

"Sit!" demanded James, pointing to Matt's previous seat, which he duly complied with.

"Right! You have clearly been the biggest tool I have ever met. I'm not going to go over everything again," started James but then his tone softened somewhat as he continued,

"Matt, mate, you have been a good friend to me over the years and I just can't believe you would have been so stupid, so reckless, by putting my life but more importantly, Adam's life in danger. I understand now, that you were under pressure and you were under a lot of stress but it still doesn't excuse your actions and I'm not even going to comment on the Daly incident but if what you say about the phone call is true, then I'll let that slide. I'm just... well disappointed. You let me down. For now, I'm not going to say anything to anyone but what you HAVE to do, is go and see Kusemi in Palma prison, tell him what you've done, arrange for this Russian hitman to get off my back and give him back his bloody money. Now can I trust you to do that?" asked James.

42

"I was planning to sort this out with Danny tomorrow, even before you said anything and before the Russian guy called here last night, I promise you. I am going to see him during visiting hours, between nine and eleven am tomorrow. James, I am so, so sorry. I never meant for you or Charlotte or the boys to get involved in any of this. I will put this right. I will come and see you tomorrow, once I've seen him. OK?" asked Matt, tentatively.

"OK," said James, as Matt made his way to the door. As Matt opened the door to leave, James added, "Oh and Matt... don't let me down again," before turning and walking away.

Chapter 4

Oh Danny Boy, No Longer

The temperature gauge in the car showed 29 degrees Celsius and it was not yet 10 o'clock, as Matt pulled into the car park of Palma prison. It was going to be a hot one, in more ways than one. It was unusually hot for mid-September. He parked his car and stepping out from his air-conditioned vehicle, the ferocity of the sun enveloped him, in an all-encompassing wave of stifling heat. Trying to walk within the shade provided by a metal canopy, which covered some of the parking spaces, he walked towards the entrance to the prison. As he did so, he was trying to think of just what to say to someone, who had been 14 years old, the last time he had seen him, apart from a fleeting glimpse of Danny Kusemi, the man, six weeks previously in Fornalutx, on that fateful night.

Matt followed the directional signs displayed in Spanish, directing visitors to the main entrance and was buzzed in through heavy steel and glass doors, which were covered by a plethora of CCTV cameras.

He approached a prison guard, who was sitting behind what appeared to be bulletproof glass. The guard looked up from his desk as he approached and Matt informed him that he had come to see Danny Kusemi. He was ushered towards two other armed prison guards and after emptying his pockets and placing the contents in a tray, he received a very thorough body search, the like of which he had not experienced, since his days as a journalist in Belfast during 'The Troubles'. He showed his photo ID and signed into a register, before being directed through a metal detector and onwards towards another door, which was opened by another guard. He was then walked down a corridor and into a large room, where inmates were already in conversation with their visitors. He was finally shown to a table and told to sit down.

He had been in prisons in N. Ireland on several occasions, when he had interviewed both Republican and Loyalist prisoners, for news pieces on paramilitary prisoners, for *The Belfast Telegraph* and for a television documentary. He wasn't nervous about the environment but rather about the person he was about to see. Matt had tried to put his past behind him for over 25 years but now that past was catching up with him.

The door to the visitation room opened and a guard walked to his table with Danny Kusemi behind. Danny looked at Matt blankly and he then looked at the guard, who indicated for him to sit, which he did, as the guard moved back towards the door.

"Do you not recognise me Danny?" asked Matt.

Kusemi's eyes were squinting as he stared directly into Matt's, before he shook his head.

"Matt Smith is what I was told. I have no fucking idea who you are. Perhaps you would be kind enough to enlighten me."

"I may have changed my surname but have I really changed that much from the boy you knew in Salter Road?"

Kusemi leaned forward in his chair, staring intently at Matt, before clearly recognising his old friend and saying,

"I don't fucking believe it! Mattie? Is that you? What the fuck are you doin' here? I haven't seen you since you did that stretch at Feltham. You know, I never really got a chance to thank you for what you did for me. Fuck me, I can't believe it! I would give you a fucking hug but they don't allow physical contact, the useless dagos. So, come on, tell me, how did you know I was in here?" said Kusemi, shaking his head in disbelief and smiling broadly.

"Oh Danny boy, Danny boy. Where do I begin? Alright. When I came out of Feltham, I didn't want to go back to Rotherhithe. I had been given a second chance. I don't regret what I did to Cheesey, because what he did to you was out of order. I knew if I went back to my old life, I would just end up like my old man or dead. I met some people, good people who believed in me, so I ended up going up North. I even ended up becoming a bloody journo, would you believe! I'm married with three great boys and I live here on the island."

"Good for you mate. I'm fucking well chuffed for you," interjected Kusemi.

"To be honest Danny, I have tried to keep my past a secret from my wife and boys and so I was pretty shocked to see you come out of a house in Fornalutx late one night, a couple of months ago."

"That was you? Fuck me! I knew someone had seen me but I thought it was just some pissed up tourist. Right, so I get it. That's how you knew where to find me," said Kusemi, still looking perplexed as to why Matt was there.

"Look Danny, your mate Daly was going to lend me some money. I needed it for my business. I had no idea of who he was, or that he had anything to do with you, until I saw you that night and I put two and two together. The reason I am here, is not to play catch up with an old friend who I haven't seen for over 25 years. I am here because I did something stupid and I have got a friend involved in this, who does not deserve what has happened to him. You know who I'm talking about: James Gordon."

"Forget it," said Kusemi, standing up and motioning to the prison guard that he wanted to leave, "I am not going to talk about that cunt! I have a boy too and it was your mate who has fucked me over big time. My boy doesn't want to know me, so it was nice to see you Mattie. See you in another 25 years, yeah."

"Danny, sit down, please. If what I did for you all those years ago means anything to you, just sit down and hear me out. I think you owe me that at least. Please."

Kusemi ushered the guard away and he retook his seat at the table.

"Right, let's have it then," he said, folding his arms.

"After you left Daly in a bad way in his house, I went in. He told me about the money and the key and that James inadvertently had the key in his possession. In a moment of madness, I tried to finish what you had started but I came to my senses and he was still alive, just about. I called an ambulance but I don't think they got enough information. Either way, we know Daly died. Whether that is down to you or me or both, it doesn't matter. You are in here for his murder and for what happened next. I am here because you need to know that James Gordon is a good guy. He's my friend, just like I considered you a friend all those years ago and he has not got the remainder of the money; I have. As you know, it wasn't James at the handover. It was me. I am the one responsible for shorting you on the cash, not him. He didn't deserve you trying to kill him in his home or for that matter, sending some Russian stooge round to put the frighteners on him. I am the one you should be mad at, not him."

"It still doesn't square things with my son though, does it?"

"Oh come on Danny. All James did, was let your boy know who the real Danny Kusemi is. He would have found out for himself sooner or later, so you can't blame James for how you turned out."

"So what do you want me to do then? I am in the shit with 'The Ruskies' at home. These guys don't take no for an answer. If I don't give them £1 million, I am dead and as far as they are concerned, they have been told your mate has got most of my money, soon to be their money. If they don't get the cash, they will be after their pound of flesh."

"Right, so you call off the Russian dogs and, in return, I will give you back the rest of your money that I have and whatever the shortfall you will have to sort that out yourself. What about the £100k that you got at the handover? Where did you put that?" asked Matt.

"It's in a safe place. Well, if you have got, say £600k or so, plus mine, that may be enough for them not to snuff me in here and I can try and get Kingpin to sort out the rest. Alright mate, this is what I'm gonna do for you and your mate. I will speak to Ale Boris but he's a fucking nutter, so I can't say he will oblige, but I'll do my best. I will need you to meet him and hand over the money you have got and I will tell you how to get the other £100k of mine. What I need you to do, is to come back here tomorrow with a SIM card for me. Can you do that for me?"

"I can but are they not going to confiscate it?" asked Matt.

"You don't fucking tell them about it, you muppet. You have to stick it up your arsehole and then ask to use the toilet before you see me to get it out. Right?"

"OK. I suppose I can try that. Until tomorrow then," said Matt, standing up. He put his hand out to shake Kusemi's hand in agreement.

"Don't do that. They'll think you are passing me something," said Kusemi, shaking his head.

Matt quickly dropped his hand and walked towards the guard, who was giving him a rueful look but who then escorted him back to the reception area and before long, Matt was walking back to his car.

As soon as he got into his car, he immediately put the aircon on full blast and sat in a reflective mood, going over what had just happened. His meeting with Danny seemed to have been over in a flash. It seemed surreal to him. He was sitting in his car, in the car park of Palma prison, just having had a conversation about a murder and a large amount of cash with a guy, who was a major drug distributor and an all-round gangster, who he had been close to over 25 years previously. He had even served a short sentence for him in a juvenile detention centre. After 25 years of being free from these sort of people and the world in which they operated, Matt hoped he was not going to be inexorably drawn back into this murky world of criminality. He had been spawned from just such beginnings and he was desperate not to let it poison the lives of his family.

He reversed out of his parking space and set off back on the road to Soller. He was not out of the woods yet. He had to make sure Danny got a SIM card, collect all the money and arrange a meeting to hand it over to a Russian, who he had been told by Danny, was a psychopathic killer. He was still battling with his conscience, over keeping his past a secret from his family and there was the moral question of whether he had been responsible for, or at least had contributed to, a man's death. On top of all this, he still had the stress of knowing that unless he had some capital injection into his business, he would have no source of income to support his family. Life for him, right at that moment, couldn't be much worse, unless he threw into the mix that he had let a good friend down, nearly getting him killed and putting his friend's family in mortal peril.

On the drive back, Matt resolved to try and make the most of a bad situation and to try and come out the other side with some remnants of dignity. He had to put things right and he now had a chance to prove his moral fabric. He emerged through the Soller tunnel with a new, determined mindset. He was now master of his own destiny and only he could fix the problems that had befallen him.

The following morning, he returned to Palma prison with the SIM card secreted in an orifice. The trick, he had been told, was not to show nerves and to be as confident as possible. 'Easier said than done,' he thought, as he received a rigorous pat down for the second time in two days. He tried to make a joke with the guard in Spanish but the joke didn't seem to go down well or was lost in translation but either way, he felt he had been close to scoring an own goal, by stepping out of his comfort zone. Fortunately, he was shown into the visitation room without any incident, for him only to then remember he still needed to remove the deposited item and quickly asked to use the toilet. The guard showed him to the visitors' toilet, following him inside. Matt went into a cubicle and locked the door. He had placed the SIM card inside a condom and tied some string to it, to aid its retrieval. He managed to recover his contraband quickly and emerged with the item hidden in a pocket. He then returned to the visitation room, with the guard none the wiser and waited for Danny.

Right on cue, Danny was deposited on the opposite side of his table and the guard retreated to the entrance.

"Well?" asked Danny, as he sat down, whilst giving a cursory glance towards the guard. "Do you have it?" he whispered.

"Yep. I've got it. So how do we do this?" asked Matt, furtively.

"Drop it on the floor and pass it over but keep your foot on it. I'll do the rest."

Matt casually dropped the condom on the floor and pushed it slowly towards his accomplice. He felt

Danny's foot touch his, at which point he recoiled his foot back and he watched as Danny dropped his cigarette packet, that he had placed on the edge of the table and he bent down to pick it up.

"Sorted?" asked Matt.

Danny nodded gently.

"So what happens now?" asked Matt, relieved that he had managed to offload his contraband.

"I have already bought 10 minutes use of a mobile phone in here but I needed the SIM. I will ring Ale Boris. I am going to get him to meet you at the pony trap racing stadium tonight at 8pm. I can see the stadium from my cell and I know the races are on tonight. I need you to take all the cash you have to the stadium tonight. My money is still in the bag you left at the handover. I placed it in a derelict little outhouse under some planks. The outhouse is about 100 metres up a lane directly opposite a school called The Academy, not far from where we had the handover. The area starts with M and has an X in it."

"Marratxi, that's where the school is. I know it," said Matt.

"OK then. You go and get that too and take it all to Ale Boris tonight, yeah? Do you know what he looks like?"

"I got a brief look at him at James' hotel opening. I think I would remember him."

"Just in case, I'll get him to wear a red baseball cap. But he's pretty much taller than any dago who goes to the races, so there shouldn't be any fuck ups, right?"

"Right."

"I'll ring my main man Kingpin, back on my manor and get him to speak to Ale Boris' boss and tell him, no

I need him to ask him, to give me more time on the rest. Do this tonight without any fuck ups and both you and your 'Old Bill' mate James are in the clear. Are we sweet Mattie?" asked Kusemi.

"We're sweet," replied Matt.

"Well then, you might as well fuck off then, as the sooner I get the hold of Ale Boris and Kingpin, the sooner I can rest a bit easier in here."

"Wish me luck," said Matt, as he stood up.

"It's not luck you need my son, it's balls and fucking brains, to make sure this goes without any more cock ups, yeah?" replied Kusemi, motioning to the guard that he had finished.

Matt waited until Kusemi was ushered away and soon he was escorted back through security and was once again reacquainted with the heat of the midday sun. He got into the oven that was his car and set off in the direction of Marratxi, on the outskirts of Palma. He drove to the entrance of The Academy School, parked his car and walked down the lane Danny had told him about, until he came to the derelict outbuilding. With no one in sight, he entered and recovered the familiar bag he had been charged with handing over to Kusemi, several months previously. Checking inside, he satisfied himself that the £100k was present and correct and returned to his car. He then drove onwards to the tunnel and through it into The Soller Valley and then on to Port de Soller and home.

Matt re-entered the tunnel just as the digital clock on his dashboard changed to 7.30pm. He placed his bankcard into the machine on exiting the tunnel, from which it debited the sum of €1.30 each time he left or re-entered the valley. It was a bit of a bugbear for him, as right now, every cent counted and he felt indignant towards the company who operated the tunnel. When he had first moved to the valley, all residents of the valley had been reimbursed annually, what they had paid to come and go. In recent years, this reimbursement had stopped. 'It could have been worse', he thought. 'At least residents of the valley pay a subsidised rate. Everyone else, whether resident on the island outside of the valley or tourists were robbed of over €5 each way'. The cost of creating the tunnel years previously, obviously had to be recouped and there were on-going running costs but it felt to him that the Madrid-based company had been given a licence to print money and despite the odd demonstration locally, he felt this monopoly would not be broken, any time soon.

He returned to the more serious matter in hand and drove on past Palmanyola and headed towards the pony and trap stadium, known as El Trot at the Hipadrom, just opposite the prison on the outskirts of Palma. He parked the car and checked the time. It was now 7.50pm. He had ten minutes to kill. He tried listening to 80s hits on a local English language radio station, Radio One Mallorca but he couldn't relax, so he alighted from his car and popped the boot. He went to the rear of his car and removed a black rucksack and relocked it. He then walked towards the entrance of the stadium with the rucksack over his right shoulder, gripping it tightly and entered the stadium through what appeared to be the only open entrance/exit. After paying a small entrance fee, he scanned the arena. A race had just finished and the result and the betting odds were being announced over the public address system. It was busier than he thought.

He estimated that a crowd of 400 people, mostly Mallorcan men were enjoying the races.

He then caught sight of a man, a third of the way round the oval track from him, wearing a red baseball cap. The man was noticeably taller than those around him and even from the distance of perhaps 200 metres, Matt was sure that this was his contact, the Russian called Ale Boris. He had enquired as to how a Russian hitman got to become known as Ale Boris and was told, by Danny, that after he had joined some of his Srebrenica Bosnian Serbs, who were working for the Russian mafia in London, that he acquired a penchant for Greene King IPA bitter and hence got the name Ale Boris.

Danny had been kind enough also to inform Matt that Ale Boris was, in Danny's words, 'A fucking nutter and a killing machine', which Matt felt was rich coming from him. He had also learned that he had taken part in The Srebrenica Massacre, in Bosnia, when thousands of Muslim men and boys were slaughtered, some of whom were Boris' own neighbours and family. He had caught the eye of the leader, General Mladic, for his barbarity and so, he, along with some ruthless Serbian fighters, called The Scorpions, were given cash rewards and after the conflict, were the first to be recruited by some of the Russian mafia, already ensconced in the criminal underworld in London.

Matt now noted, that the man in the red baseball cap was slowly walking towards him and was looking at him. He could see a bar a few feet from him and decided to head there and order a cold beer, allowing Ale Boris time to get to his position. He ordered a 'cana'; a small draft beer. As he turned to walk back towards the track, his hand was nudged by a stocky man of about thirty years of age, who must have been standing directly behind him and he appeared to be with two other men of a similar size and age. Half the contents of Matt's beer spilled over the light blue T-shirt of the man, instantly darkening the whole front of it.

"Oh, lo siento!" said Matt, apologizing for his act, albeit, that he felt the fault lay squarely with his new acquaintance.

The man looked down at his T-shirt and back at Matt and uttered the word,

"Cono!" and before he had time to react, Matt received a hard punch, which connected cleanly against the side of his jaw, sending him reeling backwards up against the bar. This made him drop his glass, which smashed on impact with the ground and allowing his rucksack to dislodge itself from over his shoulder and it ended up on the ground, to his right. He felt dazed by the blow and before his head cleared, other blows were followed up by the aggressor and his two companions. Matt put his arms up to protect his head, from what was now, a continuous onslaught of punches to his head and body. He crouched down to protect his midriff and still the blows continued and which were hard enough to knock him off his feet and onto the ground on his back. This was quickly followed up with a reign of kicks, directed at his groin area. The kicks only stopped when, despite his foetal-like position, he could hear shouts in Spanish but more enthusiastic shouts of "Leave him!" in English. He could feel the warm trickle of blood coming from his nose and his sight was becoming impaired in his right eye. He realised that a fully connecting blow to his right eye, was now making it swell up like a balloon and was quickly in danger of closing.

The shouting in English grew louder and got closer and then he realised that the orator had run past him. He slowly picked himself up and was soon assisted by two older Spanish men. Matt's head was spinning and throbbing. His eye was pounding and he felt nauseous. He placed his right arm on the bar and lifted his head up. He knew he was concussed. The barman who had served him his beer, swiftly presented him with a liberal measure of Mallorcan brandy and motioned for him to drink it, which he did. He could hear some of the Spanish men talking about ringing the police, to which he quickly said,

"No passenada!"

The last thing he wanted was the police to get involved and to start asking why he was there. Matt's clarity of vision became somewhat restored in his left eye and he could see the outline of a tall man carrying a red baseball was approaching him. It was Ale Boris. He didn't look happy and he was out of breath.

"I chased them but they got into a car and got away. What happened?" he asked.

Matt put his hand to his tender jaw, before saying,

"I turned around with my beer and he was so close, it spilled over him and the next thing I know is, he and his two mates are trying to knock seven bells out of me!"

Matt looked down at the ground and then all around him. The rucksack was gone.

"Oh shit!" he exclaimed, "They've taken my rucksack."

Ale Boris leaned in close to Matt and said, "Are you telling me they have got my boss' money?"

Matt nodded slowly.

"Fuck!" he yelled, followed by a string of words, which Matt presumed were in Bosnian.

Ale Boris approached Matt for a second time, grabbing him by the throat, causing his head to look upwards, directly into his fearsome, anger-filled eyes.

"You and Kusemi are dead men!" he spat out with venom, before releasing his vice-like grip and walked off in the direction of the exit with purpose.

Matt sank to his knees in despair. He was hurting from a savage beating and to top it all he had now been threatened by a psychopathic Bosnian hitman. 'Could his life get any worse?' he thought. He got to his feet and shuffled away from the bar, spitting out blood-stained saliva as he went. The two older Spaniards who had helped him to his feet, were protesting at him leaving, but he assured them he was fine and he continued slowly back to his car. He opened the driver's door and delicately manoeuvred himself into his seat. He pulled down his sun visor to reveal the full extent of the mess they had made to his face.

"Oh shit!" he said, at the revelation of the full horror of his injuries. 'How am I going to explain this to Jayne?' he thought. 'How am I going to explain this to Danny?'

Matt took some tissues from the glove compartment of the car and attempted to stem the flow of blood from above his right eye and from his nose. He took a few moments just to appreciate the enormity of what had just happened and then started the engine and drove back through the tunnel.

Chapter 5

Forecast: Rough,
with Pressure Rising

Matt put his key in the door to his apartment and stepped inside. It appeared that Jayne and his sons were out. He breathed a sigh of relief and went straight to the bathroom and switched on the light. He instantly got the full picture, in glorious technicolour, of the state of his face. 'Maybe I could get a job as a John Merrick, The Elephant Man, impersonator', he sarcastically thought to himself. He looked under the wash hand basin and retrieved some cotton wool balls. He then filled the sink with tepid water, whilst tentatively removing his bloodstained T-shirt, revealing reddening of his skin to one side, where he had been punched and kicked. He dabbed the congealed blood above his eye gently and removed the crusty blood clots from both nostrils and then carefully placed his head in the water.

'What was he going to tell Jayne?' he pondered.

He tended to his injuries and put on a clean T-shirt and went to the freezer, in search of a bag of frozen peas. He placed the bag over his right eye and sat down on the living room sofa, to await the return of his family.

An hour or so later, Matt heard the communal hall entry door open and the sound of his son's voices. The key turned and his front door opened and in walked his three sons, followed by Jayne. The boys went straight to their rooms, to engage with some devices with screens, which was the norm, without even noticing their father on the sofa. Jayne, however wasn't even through the door before she said,

"Oh my God Matt! What's happened?"

Jayne approached him with a look of horror on her face, which Matt could see out of his good eye.

"I'm alright, I'm alright!" he protested, "Just sit down, will you? I don't want to scare the boys."

"Well, tell me what the hell has happened then?" said Jayne, incredulous to the fact that he was alright. Her eyes were telling her something different.

"Look. It's no big deal, OK? I got beaten up by some guys when I spilled a drink over one and he completely lost his rag."

"Lost his rag? He's made a complete mess of your face. You need to go to hospital. That cut above your eye needs stitches. Oh I can't look at that! Your eye! You can hardly see out of it. Where did this happen?"

"At a little bar at Poligano de Son Castello. I was doing a sign for a client and stopped for a quick beer, when these guys bumped into me and this is the result."

"Have you reported it to the Police?"

"No, there's no point. No one else was there; even the barman had gone out to change a barrel, so there is no point in reporting it. Look, I'll be fine in a day or two and I don't want to go to hospital. I just need a good night's sleep. Please stop worrying. OK?" said Matt.

"Unbelievable! In this day and age you can't go for a quiet drink, without some stupid macho man trying to make me a widow! Alright, rant over. Oh, Matt, look at the state of you love. Can I do anything for you?" said Jayne, sympathetically.

"No, no thanks pet. I just need to get to bed. Night, night."

Matt went to bed and was later joined by Jayne. He pretended to be asleep when she turned in but in truth, he lay awake for several hours, worrying what was going to happen next and due to the pain he was suffering from his injuries but he eventually feel asleep.

He spent the next morning in bed, not wishing to get up to face the consequences of the previous evening's incident, but his lie-in was interrupted, when Jayne entered the bedroom with the phone.

"James is on the phone for you. I told him about last night and he wants a word," she said, handing the phone to Matt, before leaving.

"Hi James," said Matt.

"What happened?" asked James, in a concerned voice.

"Oh mate," sighed Matt, "I went to the meet, as planned, and I could see your Russian, who incidentally is Bosnian, and I went to get a quick beer and before I knew it, some idiot had bumped into me and the next thing is, he and his two mates are kicking the crap out of me. Ale Boris chased them but they got away. They also got my rucksack and the money."

"They got the money? What, all of it?" James asked, incredulously.

"Yes. Every last note. I'm lying here with one eye swollen closed, a possible broken nose and from the pain I still have this morning, possibly fractured ribs."

"Have you told Kusemi what happened yet?"

"I haven't had a chance to. I'll go and see him later. The thing is, Ale Boris saw the whole thing but I have to tell you James, he was pretty angry. Until I see Kusemi and try and square things with him, just be a bit extra careful."

"Oh great! So now you're telling me that I'm still in the shit with the Russians. Great! I thought you squared things with Kusemi about me already?"

"I did! I did! It's just as a precaution," pleaded Matt.

"What was the last thing I said to you when I saw you? I said, Matt don't let me down again. What have you done?"

"Oh come on James, that isn't fair! How was I supposed to know that three arseholes would pick a fight with me and then take the money? No, that's not fair. If you saw the state of me here, I don't think you'd be so unsympathetic. Look, I will see Kusemi shortly and he will just have to sort this out with the Russians. His guys in London are still bringing home the bacon, so I'm sure he can get more money to cover his debt. I'm trying to sort this whole mess out James... just cut me some slack!" said an exasperated Matt.

"Alright. Just ring me when you've spoken to Kusemi. OK?" said James.

"Fine. Fine, OK. I'll ring you later. Bye," replied Matt.

A few hours later Matt made his way back to Palma prison to face the music with Danny.

Kusemi was escorted to the visitation room and deposited in front of Matt. Kusemi looked concerned.

"What the fuck happened to you? Did Boris get the money?" he asked, anxiously.

"Before you blow your top, no, Boris did not get the money. I picked up your £100k and added it to the remainder and placed it in my rucksack. I got to the stadium in good time and walked in and I saw Ale Boris in the distance. He saw me and I thought it would look better if we did the handover at the bar, so I got a drink and was turning round to see where Boris was, when some idiot spilled my drink over himself. I apologised but the next thing I know is that he and his two mates are knocking seven bells out of me. Boris can verify this. I mean... look at the state of me. Do you think I enjoy getting used as a punch bag? Anyway, I was knocked to the ground and I can hear Boris shouting at them. When I get back to my feet, I notice the rucksack was gone. Now, I'm not necessarily blaming Boris for taking the bag, but it's possible. It is more likely that the three Spaniards saw their chance to nick my bag, without realising what was in it. The other possibility, although I can't give you anything to back it up, is that I was set up. It is possible, is it not, that Boris had these guys in place and when he saw me, he gave them the nod and they did the business. He makes it out to his boss and to you that he didn't get the money, when all along he's sitting pretty?" said Matt.

"It's possible," surmised Kusemi, rubbing his chin, deep in thought. "There is one other explanation of what happened of course…"

"Don't even go there!" interrupted Matt. "Do you think I would be stupid enough to try anything and then for a laugh, get my face beaten to a pulp? Yeah, I knew you would try and place the blame at my door. Well, I'm not having it, right! I could have quite easily kept the money I had and not come anywhere near you but I stuck my head above the parapet to help a friend and I gave up any right to that money in order to do so. I told him about my past and risked him telling my wife and came here to meet up with you after 25 years, after I had put all that behind me and now you sit there accusing me! Well you can go and fuck yourself Danny!" spouted Matt, as he stood up to leave.

"Alright! Alright! Don't have a fucking coronary! Sit down, I believe you. Come on, sit down," said Kusemi, motioning with his hand.

Matt returned to his chair and sat down.

"Look, I have to look at it from all angles. What did Ale Boris say to you?"

"He said that you and I were dead men and then left, basically."

"Fuck sake. Listen, you watch your back. I am going to try and sort this with his boss. I will get Kingpin, who works for me, to pay him a visit, with a down payment. He will just have to wait a bit longer than he likes, if he wants to get paid at all. What's your mobile number?"

"Why?"

"Because I want to use it for this week's lottery numbers. So as I can ring you to tell you if it's sorted or not. You do want to know if I can get you out of the fucking shit or not, don't you?" said Kusemi, shaking his head.

"But how will you remember it if I tell you?" asked Matt.

"Let me fucking worry about that. Didn't you know I have got a photographic memory?"

"No, I didn't. What a waste, if that's true. Anyway the number is 634 391040. Got it?"

"Yeah I got it, 634 391040. No problem. Right, you fuck off and I'll call you either way. You send a boy to do a man's job, eh? I don't know if you could have hacked it, if you'd come back to your old life. Perhaps it was best you didn't," said Kusemi, shaking his head with a rueful grin and standing up to be taken back to his cell.

Matt left a short time later and rang James on his way home to inform him of how the meeting went. He spent the next two days recuperating at home and had no further contact with James. As he was getting ready for bed, his mobile phone rang. The number was withheld.

"Hello."

"Told you I'd remember it, didn't I?" came the now familiar voice of Danny Kusemi. "I'll be brief. My man Kingpin has come up with two hundred grand as a down payment to Boris's boss. You're off the hook. Your mate is off the hook and with any luck I'll be fucking off the hook. Boris has gone back to London. Anyway, I thought you should know. Now we're even, yeah. See you Mattie boy."

The call was over in a flash but Matt felt a wave of relief flow over him. He could have cried. A huge weight had been lifted from his shoulders. He immediately rang James.

"James, it's me. I've just had a call from Kusemi. He's sorted it. He has made a down payment to the Russians and he's going to pay them off over time. We are out of the loop. The Russians won't touch us and obviously Danny won't touch you. It's over mate."

"Thank God for that. You are sure that's it?" asked James.

"As sure as you can be with these people. Any thoughts on the other issue?"

"If you're referring to Daly, I still haven't checked about your call. I will need to ask Martinez to do it. He's going to wonder why I'm interested but I'll just say it was in my dream or something. Until then, I'm saying nothing. I won't do anything without talking to you first. I owe you that, at least," responded James.

"OK. Well, I appreciate that. Take care. Bye."

With that, Matt hung up and went to bed, feeling he could sleep more soundly than over the previous few nights.

A few days later, James asked Inspector Martinez, as a personal favour to him, to check if any calls to 112 had been made around one am on the night of Daly's murder. He was curious as to the request but James said that perhaps Kusemi had rung and that he just felt it in his gut. A week later James received a call from Martinez confirming that a call was received at about 1.15am on the night of the murder, from a pay as you go mobile phone and through triangulation from mobile phone masts, he was able to conclude that the call had been made from Fornalutx.

"The caller said; "There's a man..." in English, and that's all that was received. It could have been Kusemi but without voice recognition, it's hard to tell and anyway, what does it add to the case? Do you think it was Kusemi?" asked Martinez.

"Yes. I think he got cold feet and left him still alive and thought he would give his old friend another chance. Bam Bam told me that Kusemi seemed surprised that Daly's death was from asphyxiation or perhaps just that he had died, having rung for an ambulance," said James, trying to throw Martinez off the scent of anyone else being involved. He had concluded, on receipt of this information, that he would not ruin the lives of not only Matt but those of his family, by disclosing any information to either Martinez or to Jayne.

James thanked Ramon for the information and immediately rang Matt, to inform him of what he had discovered and to reaffirm that he would not reveal any information to Jayne or Martinez. Matt couldn't hide his relief and was very thankful to him but James was matter-of-fact and brusque and ended the call, telling Matt that he needed some space for a while, to reflect on everything that had happened. Matt agreed.

Chapter 6

Never a Dull Moment

The days soon turned into weeks and James had been distracted by running his hotel. Bookings had been better than he had expected and it was now the end of October and his little, six bedroomed hotel was booked right up to the middle of November. He had not been in contact with Matt throughout this time but had seen Jayne in the local supermarket and enquired after him and was told that he was well and quite busy with his sign-writing business. Charlotte had mellowed over the weeks since their visit from Ale Boris and although she still brought it up from time to time, James had assured her that Kusemi had now stopped his campaign of seeking some form of retribution against him. Martinez had come back to him with an update regarding the forensic examination of the bullet. It was, as James suspected, clean but he had placed the suspect, Dzan Kovacavevic aka Ale Boris, on a wanted list for the offence.

James had got into the routine of assisting Charlotte in preparing their guests' continental breakfasts in the morning and sharing the duty of manning the hotel reception desk during the day. Reuben and Adam were back at school and Adam had settled back into a normal life, despite having had two minor lapses in the form of nightmares, regarding his ordeal at the hands of Kusemi. Charlotte had arranged for him to see a counsellor, specialising in child psychology, in the coming days.

James was at the reception desk, when a couple of his guests from Rutland, who were on a house-buying trip, came back to the hotel.

"Well, did everything go to plan?" he enquired of the couple, who were due to complete on the purchase of a holiday apartment in Port de Soller.

"I'm afraid not, James," said Mike.

"What happened?" asked James showing concern, walking from behind the reception desk.

His wife, Maggie was crying.

"We've just spent the last hour at the local Police station in Soller, giving a statement. We weren't able to complete the purchase, as we were robbed outside the notary's office, just before we were due to complete on the apartment. I was knocked to the ground by some guy in a motorbike helmet and he stole the envelope I had on me, which contained €40,000 in 'black money' that I had in cash, at the behest of the seller."

"Are you OK?" said James, putting his hand on Mike's shoulder to console him.

"As well as you can be after being robbed. What I keep asking myself is, how they knew I would be there at that particular time, with that sort of money on me?"

"What did the police say?"

"We had to wait for a detective. He says he knows you. I have his card here. Inspector Ramon Martinez," he read from the card.

"Yes. I know Ramon. He's a good guy. What did he tell you?" asked James.

"Well, he said that this was the third incident of this type in Soller over the last few months and the description of the suspects was similar. He didn't say much else, other than they would do their best to catch these guys. Anyway, we couldn't complete the purchase as I haven't got a spare €40,000 to hand. We are now having second thoughts about buying here at all, even though we may end up losing our deposit," said Mike, comforting his wife.

"Oh, I'm so sorry to hear that. If I can be of any help, just let me know. I will speak to Inspector Martinez to see if I can find out anything more for you."

"Thanks James. I'd appreciate that," he said, as he and his wife returned to their room.

James checked some new guests into their room and then drove to Palma later in the day to collect Adam and two other children of friends from Soller, from their international school before returning home. After the evening meal, he rang Ramon regarding the robbery of his unfortunate guests.

"Hey Ramon. It's James. You've had a busy day?" enquired James.

"Hola James. Yes, so you've heard the news? This is the third incident with a similar pattern over the last few months. We are following up some leads but we don't have much to go on. It appears your guests today, like the previous two times, were ready to go into the notary's office, to sign for the deeds to a house.

In all cases, like a lot of house sales here in Mallorca, the seller had requested a percentage of the deal to be in 'black money' and either the robbers have inside information or they have been lucky in that, in all three attacks, they have all been carrying a large sum of cash."

"Is there any pattern of similar use of estate agent or solicitor or something?"

"There is no clear pattern. The three victims were British, Swedish and German. Each used a different inmobiliaria and only one used a lawyer. The notary office staff have been there for years, in fact one is related to me. I am satisfied they have nothing to do with this. We have looked at who is living in the street and all are locals with no previous convictions and a couple of flats are let out to tourists. The moped used has been described just as a white Vespa-type moped but one distinctive thing that your guy today spotted, was a round or an oval sticker on the rear number plate. There are two robbers, both with black, full-face crash helmets but the description of the clothing changes each time. They have both been described as heavy build and heights vary between 1.7 metres and 2 metres. We have asked our bosses to put a plain-clothes unit in a flat above the notary's office but we do not have the manpower at the moment. That's all I can tell you at the minute James."

"Thanks for that Ramon. If I hear anything, I'll let you know. Cheers."

James walked the few steps to his hotel next door and went to the first floor room and knocked the door. He could hear someone stir inside, before the door was opened by Mike, the earlier victim of the robbery.

"I'm sorry to disturb you Mike, but I just wanted to check if you and Maggie are feeling any better?"

"Come in, come in James," said Mike, ushering him inside. "To be honest, we have been having a bit of a siesta. We had a stiff G & T when we got back."

The bathroom door opened and Maggie returned to the main bedroom and greeted James, before sitting in an armchair.

"I just wanted to tell you, that I have spoken to Inspector Martinez. He's a friend of mine. I don't think I've told you this but I used to be a Detective myself quite a few years ago, so I understand what you are going through. I know it's not much consolation but at least you were not seriously, physically hurt. It is a large amount of money for anyone to lose but you can replace money. You can't replace people. Ramon has told me they are working hard to try and establish a clear link with all three attacks. Obviously, it appears they have been carried out by the same guys but we still can't, listen to me, I should say, they still can't work out how they got lucky three times out of three. I could understand if there had been other similar robberies of people in the same area, who hadn't got 'black money' in large amounts on them but there haven't been. Anyway, I'm really sorry this has happened. It is not normal for this to happen round here, I can assure you. Wait until the dust settles before you make any decision on the completion. I'm sure the vendor will allow an extended completion date after what has happened. Perhaps you might ask them to reduce the price slightly, under the circum-stances?" said James, trying to provide them with a positive outlook.

"You're right, of course, James. We were both a bit shaken up but neither of us was hurt. It could have turned out very differently. We are long enough in the tooth to realise, that this sort of thing could happen anywhere; even in beautiful Soller and that we have just been extremely unlucky. Mrs P and I will go and see our lawyer tomorrow and see what we can do, so we haven't given up on our retirement dream just yet," said Mike, taking his wife's hand to comfort her.

"That's the spirit. Oh Mike, just one other thing about today. The two suspects. Did either of them speak?"

"Not a word. One was already on a little white moped further up the street and the one who pushed me over, well, all I can say James, is he was strong. He nearly gave me whiplash, he pushed me that hard," said Mike, trying to muster a smile from his wife, without success.

"Inspector Martinez said you thought the moped had a round or oval sticker on the rear number plate. Is that right?"

"I think so. It was so far away but as the sun caught the number plate, it seemed to glisten on a small, round bit at the top and it wasn't a light cluster. Look, the grandchildren collect these stickers and they are almost like 3D. That sort of thing but I can't be sure."

"Anyway, I shall leave you in peace. You say you like gin and tonic? Please help yourselves to as much, or as little, as you want from the honesty bar, or indeed any other drinks you like, on the house. Good evening."

"Thank you James," the couple said in unison, as he left.

The next morning, James dropped Adam off in Soller at the meeting point, for him to be picked up by their friends, with whom they shared the rigours of the daily school run to Palma. Reuben would be getting the school bus from Fornalutx to Soller about now and Charlotte would be serving guests breakfast, along with their new member of staff of Hotel Artesa, Monica, a new resident of Fornalutx, originally from Romania.

James was half way to losing a stone in weight and generally making progress in toning up and keeping fit and so several weeks previously, he had joined a new gym at the new sports hall in Soller, called Son Angelats. Prior to this, he had been a member of the rather more salubrious health club and spa, at the five star Jumeirah hotel, in Port de Soller. It was luxurious and it had been great to use their facilities during the summer, with a panoramic sea view from the spa pool but it was easier for James to use the bigger gymnasium in Soller, where he was meeting locals, not just wealthy guests on holiday.

He tended to go to the gym just after eight o'clock, when he wasn't doing the morning school run to Palma, now that Monica had started at the hotel. He had been getting to know the instructors and the regular members, even just to say 'hola' to, if not yet able to have full-blown conversations with the majority of the members, who were mostly local. There were a few who were either German or British also.

He was finishing his session of weight-training and some cardio work on the running machine, about the same time as a guy, who he had noticed had become a regular at this time of morning, most mornings, for the last few weeks. He held the door open for the man, who was in his mid-thirties, quite muscular, with short, cropped black hair and he smiled at James and said

"Gracias," for his gesture. Normally, James took a shower at the venue but he noted that his new acquaintance went to the lockers in a landing area, outside the gym door and retrieved a bag and a black, full-face, crash helmet. James decided to forgo his shower and instead got his bag from his locker and followed the man out of the building, a few feet behind. He watched as the man placed his bag over his shoulder and put his crash helmet on, as he walked to where several scooters and motorbikes were parked in the allocated 'Motos' bay.

He observed, as he got astride a white Vespa scooter, which James could see had a Spanish number plate and obscuring one of the letters on the rear number plate was an oval sticker. His heart began to beat faster. He was standing about thirty feet from the back of the man now. He had left his prescription sunglasses in his car and from this distance he could not tell anything further about the sticker.

'This was too much to be a coincidence', he thought, as he quickly made his way to his car, a few feet away, just as the scooter roared off.

James hurled his bag onto the front passenger seat, spilling its contents onto the floor. He quickly started the engine and sped off in pursuit of the moped. He drew up close behind it, when the rider had to give way to traffic at the next roundabout and now, sporting his trusty prescription sunglasses, he could clearly see the sticker did indeed have a shiny, almost 3D effect outline, which glinted in the morning sunlight, as the rider traversed the roundabout and headed into Soller.

He followed at a reasonable distance, not wishing to spook the rider, who, he felt, would have seen him leave the gym car park behind him. He glanced nonchalantly from left to right every so often, in case the rider was checking him out in his wing mirrors. Adrenalin was now flowing in James' body. He felt convinced that this guy was one of the robbers of his guests. Too many things fitted for it to be a coincidence: his height, his build, his scooter, his helmet but most incriminating of all, was the sticker on his rear number plate. James fell back to about twenty feet from the scooter. He had been taught the trade craft of surveillance but it was just him on his own and he had moments earlier brought himself to the attention of a potential suspect, so by all accounts, a lot of what he had been taught had been compromised.

The scooter stopped, to allow an antique tram to pass, on its way to Port de Soller. James had no alternative but to drive up to a normal distance behind the scooter. The lights returned from red to amber again and the scooter revved and continued its journey, followed at a short distance behind, by James. The scooter then pulled in near to the covered market in Soller and down over a bridge. James knew, that the street the man would come to next was the street where the notary's office was. It was a narrow street and he felt if he too drove down it and the man saw him, it may be too suspicious. Taking a risk that the suspect may drive on through the streets beyond, he made the decision to decamp from his vehicle and abandoned it, blocking in some other parked cars. Knowing he faced the very real danger of a €150 fixed penalty ticket, for such behaviour, he threw caution to the wind and sprinted from his car to the corner of the street, just in time to see the man get off his scooter, open a set of large wooden gates and ride the scooter into an area behind the gates, which he heard him close and then bolt from the inside.

James cautiously and furtively walked up to where the gates where and looked at the house, which they evidently belonged to. The house had obviously been converted into three flats, judging by the three buzzers on the intercom and the three letterboxes outside. He looked at the house number of the three-storey, traditional, green-shuttered townhouse and saw the number 12. He looked behind him and realised that he was now standing directly opposite the notary's office.

James felt exposed. He quickly walked back towards his car, ensuring he was out of sight of any occupants of any of the three flats of number 12, as he did so. Once back around the corner, his quick walk turned into a sprint, not only as he wanted to divulge his discovery to Martinez but also with equal vigour, to stop the almost eagle-eyed predators, who were the ORA traffic wardens. He had experienced their dedication to their job on two previous occasions. The first had been, when he had unwittingly parked in an area that was reserved for council staff only, in Soller. He had parked for no more than five minutes, to go to the bank and on his return, he was welcomed by the fluttering of a pink docket under his wiper blades. On the second occasion, on a night out in Soller, he had parked the car in a designated parking bay and displayed a ticket valid until 10am the next day. As he had had a few drinks, he decided a taxi back to Fornalutx was the sensible thing to do. He noted that he was parked in front of a disabled bay and that due to the car in front taking up a little of his space, he was perhaps two inches over the line into the disabled bay. Judging that this was fine, he returned to recover his car the next morning, only to find another car in its place. He began to doubt that this was where he had parked but after several phone calls, it was established that his car had been ticketed and been lifted by the local parking 'mafia'. €230 lighter, James got his vehicle back and when asked to see the photographic evidence of his grave misdemeanour, he got so baffled with the instructions as to how to go about getting the photograph, he never followed it up.

Out of the corner of his eye, James could see that a man wearing a blue baseball cap and a 'high-vis' jacket was approaching his car. He leapt into the driver's seat, started the engine and screeched away, just as he could see the traffic warden reach for his dreaded pad. He had missed a bullet. He continued with purpose, driving back to Fornalutx and parked his car. He attempted to use the Bluetooth system in his car but every time he had been asked to say which name and he answered Ramon, the automated voice kept saying 'pardon'. After the fourth attempt, he gave up, so once parked, he picked his mobile phone off the floor in the front passenger foot well and rang Inspector Martinez.

"Hola James."

"Ramon. Listen, I think I've found one of your robbers!" James said, eagerly. "I was at the gym this morning at Son Angelats in Soller and I noticed a guy who has been a regular over the last, oh I don't know, say three months. Anyway, when he was leaving, he lifted a black full-face crash helmet and got onto a white Vespa with guess what? A round sticker on the back number plate. I followed him to his flat, which is, would you believe, directly opposite the notary's office. It has to be our man. He's about 1.8m in height, mid 30's and of muscular build," said James, hardly stopping for breath.

"James, James. Let me get a word in. That sounds promising. Well done, good work. I am not at work at the moment but I am due to start in a couple of hours. Let me get to work. I'll ring you straight away and then I'll come over to see you this evening. OK?"

"OK, Ramon. That's fine. See you later."

"Well done my friend. This work is obviously in your blood. Even if it is not our guy, you still have a gift for this work. Adios amigo."

James felt elated. He had enjoyed his investigative work in the Police but what he loved most, was chasing and arresting suspects. His work in The RUC had mostly been arranging searches or going to murder scenes and interviewing prisoners, which he had enjoyed to a certain degree but what really got his adrenaline flowing, was during his early career in uniform and later in plain clothes, as part of a Crime Team in Rotherhithe, during his days in The Metropolitan Police. The job there was always busy and arrests and chases, whether on foot or in a Police Area car, were frequent. In short, he loved the thrill of the chase.

He took a minute to compose himself but his mind was racing. He still couldn't put his finger on exactly how the suspects could get a payday out of each of the three times they had struck. Unable to come up with a satisfactory explanation, he walked home quickly and showered and awaited Martinez's phone call.

Chapter 7

The Net Closes

It was later than James expected, before Martinez finally called to tell him he was on his way, as he had wanted to brief his superior and do some research on the owners of the three flats. Half an hour later, Martinez knocked on the door to James' house.

"Come in Ramon, let's go to my study," said James, leading the way upstairs.

Both men sat down opposite each other.

"Well, what have you got?" asked James, inquisitively.

"I am assuming, until we prove otherwise, that this guy, is one of the two robbers. I am getting a surveillance unit set up in an empty office above the notary's office, to monitor the flat that I think these guys are using. They will be in position in an hour. If we were to just go in and arrest them, yes, we might find some of the money but how do we prove any money found inside is linked to the three robberies? We can't get witnesses to identify them, as they were wearing crash helmets and they changed their clothing for each robbery. Even if you are correct and the scooter does have an unusual sticker, as seen by your guest, it does not add up to enough hard evidence for the prosecutor to take them to court. I have spoken to my boss and for now, we watch them and try and catch them in the act."

"OK, Ramon. I'll leave you to get on with things. Let me know if anything happens, will you?"

"Yes, of course. You are almost part of my team now. How much do you charge for your services?" he said, jokingly.

"I'm pretty cheap; a couple of cervezas usually covers it," retorted James.

For the next two weeks, James' guests came and went, until it was now mid-November. He had arranged for the hotel to close from this period until mid-February. This was a quieter period in Mallorca generally but he noted that a few hotels were remaining open all through the year, which he commended and in due course, intended to do the same. He had wanted to get a few months experience under his belt and then have a break, as it had been quite a hectic year and he wanted to have some quality time with his family.

During the previous fortnight, he had been going to the gym in Son Angelats regularly and continued to see the suspect there most days. He had concluded that the man was Spanish or South American, as he had overheard him speak Castilliano, rather than Mallorquin. He had been in regular contact with Martinez during this period and so far, they had drawn a blank on who the men were and there had been no further robberies over the period. Martinez' boss had given him one more week and if nothing happened, Martinez would have to go in and arrest them and hope to find something incriminating in the flat. James knew, from previous experience, that this may not provide enough evidence to charge them with an offence and would simply make them shift their set up somewhere else and not necessarily put a stop to their criminality.

He had been told that the OP or observation post, that was monitoring the flat twenty-four hours a day, had identified two males who were renting a middle floor flat from a local woman for a six-month period. Enquiries had been discretely made with her and it had been discovered that the two men claimed to be from Chile and Morocco. They had given names to their landlord but had paid in cash and had not provided her with any form of photographic ID. A 'names check' came back as a 'no trace' on either man, leading all concerned to believe that they had given false names. There was nothing unusual about their behaviour since the OP had been set up and they hadn't noticeably been bringing back any high value purchases. One thing of note that Martinez had shared with James, was that the Moroccan had been observed, looking into the notary's office, using a pair of binoculars. This had almost been the undoing of the surveillance unit, whose video camera had to be further disguised, as at one point, one of the suspects seemed to be paying undue attention to the window where they had the camera set up.

The fact that the suspects were using binoculars, had led the investigators to conclude that it was just possible, that from their position overlooking the notary's office, and using what appeared to be powerful binoculars, that the suspects had been able to get sight of the notary's diary, which was kept open on his secretary's desk and would have been visible from their position.

Without the hotel to contend with, James was becoming frustrated with the lack of progress on the robbers. He decided to ring Martinez.

"Ramon. I have been thinking. I can't look at this guy at the gym every day without thinking he needs to be behind bars. He's walking around as free as a bird and he's beginning to annoy me now. He thinks he's a bit of a lad and he's been letching over some of the girls who come to the gym. It's not exactly being an agent provocateur if, let's say, you come to the gym, and tell me about your plan to buy a house say, on Thursday and he overhears the fact you will have, let's say €100k 'black money', in a shoulder bag you will be carrying. Come on Ramon, it's time you got these bastards."

"I agree with you. Let me make a phone call and I'll get back to you."

Half an hour later James' mobile rang. It was Martinez.

"Right, we are on. I had some trouble with my boss initially, as he didn't want to involve you and also he thought we might have to use real money but I told him we didn't need money to prove robbery and we should be able to tie them to the other crimes, so he said yes. I will come to your place tomorrow morning and we will go to the gym for 8.15am. If things go to plan and our man is there, I will speak to you in Spanish about me buying the house etc. Hopefully he will take the bait and with any luck, he won't be able to resist the opportunity for an easy €100k and then we'll get them both on Thursday. OK?"

"Good stuff. See you in the morning," said an excited James.

He was glad to be involved and happy to be helping to take people of their calibre off the street. He also enjoyed the legal subterfuge used to catch criminals. He had previously been involved in test purchase operations, where he had been used to buy drugs from dealers in order to build up a case against them. There were strict operational rules governing such police practices, where what you said was vitally important. Equally so, was the evidence gathering obtained by the use of pinhole cameras and sound recording equipment, which were important tools of the trade. So he went to bed fully prepared for his role the following morning.

The next morning, Martinez arrived at James' house and briefed him about the operation. Martinez was already kitted out in his gym wear and he had both sound and vision, as they felt it was good practice to record what they would say and see, for evidential purposes. James' role would be solely one of a listener, as he admitted himself that his understanding of Spanish was still in its infancy. James set off on his scooter and Martinez followed in his unmarked police car. Other officers were still in place near the notary's office. They had also made sure, that details of the alleged property purchase had been placed in the diary of the notary and left open for the robbers to see, in the hope that they were continuing with their practice of spying from their flat.

James parked up his scooter in the parking bay and noted that the white Vespa was already there.

'Good. He's here,' he thought, as he removed his helmet and walked into Son Angelats and made his way to the gym on the second floor. He continued with his routine of placing his bag in the lockers and then used his swipe card to gain entry to the gym. Knowing that Martinez did not have a membership card for entry, he took the liberty of putting a chair up against the open door, as if allowing a better flow of air into the space. No one noticed his action and he joined the half dozen other users already in, including the target.

He did some stretching exercises and a few moments later observed Martinez enter the gym. James went to the bench press machine and loaded some weights onto the barbell. After a couple of sets, he motioned with his eyes for Martinez to come closer, as the target was using an adjacent machine. Martinez approached James and asked, in Spanish, if he could do alternate sets and James agreed. The two men introduced themselves to each other and in between sets, chatted about Martinez's imminent purchase of a house in Soller the following day. James did most of the listening but could hear Martinez make a big deal of the fact that he would have €100k in cash on him in the morning and that he wasn't happy about this but that was what the seller wanted. From time to time, James glanced over at the target, who appeared to be listening to their conversation, despite the music being played in the gym that morning at a particularly loud volume. He hoped that it hadn't hindered the target hearing the pertinent parts of their conversation.

A short time later, both men watched the target leave and Martinez then left to inform his other officers. James finished off and met Martinez outside.

"Right. So now we wait until tomorrow. I will go to outside the notary's office for 11 o'clock. Everyone will be in place and then we wait. I can't get authorization for you to be there tomorrow James but if you happened to be in that general area, say around the corner near the dental surgery, well it's a free country isn't it?" said Martinez.

"I will go to the gym tomorrow morning for a little while, if you like, to see if he is there," said James.

"That's fine with me but it is best not to talk to him, just in case he starts asking you questions. I have seen defenders use such instances to get their client's off charges, where they claim they were set up. It is your normal activity, so why change it and create suspicion? See you after. Thanks for your input today. Adios."

Martinez drove off to make arrangements for the following day and James got back on his scooter and rode back to Fornalutx. He was eager to tell Charlotte what had been happening but felt that it may be yet another thing for her to worry about, so he remained silent on the subject. The village was peaceful at this time of year. There were still plenty of sunny days and walking in The Tramuntana Mountains was becoming more of a pastime for Charlotte and James. It was usually possible for them to fit in a walk once a week, now that the hotel had closed for the season. During the day, if Reuben had an after school club and Adam was collected from school by their friends, it gave them several hours to join friends on a sojourn through the mountains, on the various walking paths that dotted the area.

James loved the village and mountains at this time of year. Even though it was autumn, it didn't feel like autumn in the UK. There were very few deciduous trees in Mallorca, so you didn't get the feeling that it was autumn, due to the lack of changing leaf colours and finally the loss of leaves on the trees. The mountains were still covered with the silvery green olive trees and the pines, orange and lemon trees still provided plenty of greenery. Indeed, the orange trees were full to bursting with a bountiful array of oval tree decorations.

The village was very much a living, working village. People still went about their daily work. Most of the bars and restaurants were still open but quieter than during the long, hot summer days. This was the time of year to enjoy the natural beauty and the splendour of all the island had to offer. It was also a time to do work to properties, when at least you knew you wouldn't be soaked in sweat after ten minutes, unlike throughout the summer months. James, like many people on the island, was dependent on tourism for their way of life and in recent years, the image of Mallorca had been changing from one of a drink-fuelled party destination, as provided by places like Magaluf, to somewhere for the more discerning traveller, who enjoyed breathtaking scenery, culture, good food, architecture and a gem of a capital city, that was compact and for James, that rivalled Barcelona.

He woke early the following morning and set off a little earlier than usual for the gym on his scooter. He wasn't in the mood to be there and shortly after eight o'clock, ten minutes after his own arrival, he was joined by the target. He lifted his head in recognition and the man nodded. James did the bare minimum and then left and took a shower and got dressed. He went to the scooter bay and noticed that the target's scooter had already left. He rang Martinez to appraise him of this and wished him good luck. The time had just gone 9.30 am. It would be another hour and a half before the sting operation, so he rode into Soller and ordered a café con leche and a napolitana from Café Paris, a little café in the plaça. It was still warm enough to sit outside and enjoy the autumn sunshine and to partake in the local sport of people watching. Soller was busy with locals going about their daily routines and there were still a few intermittent hoots from the orange antique trams coming and going from the tram depot, a short distance away. After a further refill, James returned to where he had parked his scooter, put his helmet on and rode the short distance to the corner of the street where the notary's office was. He put the moped on its side stand and checked the time. It was 10.55am.

James texted Martinez, to tell him his location. His mobile vibrated to alert him that Martinez was now in place outside the notary's office. He took a deep breath. 'Here we go,' he thought. He remained out of sight of the street but he knew, if he was needed, he could run around the corner and be there in seconds. The whole area was quiet. There was no one in sight of James, other than a delivery driver offloading some kegs of beer to a café about 100 metres away towards the main street. He stood beside his scooter with his helmet on and waited and waited. He pulled his mobile from his pocket. No new messages.

All of a sudden, James could hear shouting coming from the direction of the street where Martinez was. He then heard the unmistakeable crack of gunfire; twice. He ran round the corner to see, about 200 metres away, the figure of Martinez wrestling on the ground with a man in a black crash helmet. Two other men were standing over them, pointing their police issue firearms in their outstretched hands. One of the plain-clothes officers kicked the prone suspect hard in the midriff. James could see at the far end of the street another plain-clothes officer had his firearm pointing at the second suspect on the white scooter. He was shouting at the suspect to stay where he was and to put his hands up. James had determined that the two shots he had heard, had been warning shots, discharged by police. Without warning, he heard the sound of the moped accelerate from its stationary position and go out of sight of both him and the pursuing officer. He knew these little, cobbled streets quite well, so he ran back to his scooter and gave chase via another adjoining street.

There were two possible ways the rider could have gone at the end of the street. He would have to take a guess as to his direction of travel. He went left and to the end of his street. Nothing. He got off his scooter and switched off the engine, to see if he could hear the sound of the target's moped. He could hear the sound of a moped getting closer and it was travelling fast for the narrow streets, judging by the high-pitched whirring of the engine. Thinking quickly on his feet, James looked around him for something to assist in stopping the suspect. There was nothing visible. He walked a couple of feet, to the front of a townhouse and clasped his hands round an old, green-painted, metal drainpipe and pulled hard. The bottom section of about a metre came away from the wall, just as the moped and its rider turned the corner where he was standing. Instinctively and without any thought as to the consequences of his actions, he swung the pipe back quickly and connected with helmet of the rider.

The force of the blow knocked the rider backwards off the white Vespa, which veered onto the footpath and came to an abrupt halt against the wall of a house, thirty feet or so away. The suspect was on his back. James could see that there was still slight movement from him. He was moaning, so at least he knew he hadn't killed him. He had never used unreasonable force in his time as a police officer, even though there were many times, when force had been necessary. He had never had to hit any suspect with a drainpipe before, so he was trying to work out in his head, whether a court would view this as reasonable force in Spain.

Whilst keeping an eye on the suspect on the ground, he started to get his mobile out, to inform Martinez of his whereabouts but returned it to his pocket, when running footsteps he heard got louder and soon, standing in front of him was one of Martinez's plain-clothes officers, who recognised James from an earlier briefing. The plain-clothes officer leaned over the suspect, who was obviously the Moroccan, judging from the glimpses of dark flesh he could see and placed handcuffs on the prisoner. He then radioed for assistance and a short time later, the whole street was awash with police. Martinez entered the street and approached James.

"Give me your hand," said Ramon, as he offered an outstretched hand.

James obliged and Ramon shook his hand firmly.

"I just wanted to shake the hand of the mastermind who almost single-handedly solved the case by himself!" said Martinez, smiling broadly at James.

"Oh come on! You guys did all the work. I was just happy to help," said James, looking down at the Moroccan, as they removed his crash helmet. He was extremely dazed and didn't seem to know where he was.

"He will have a sore head in the morning!" laughed Martinez and grabbing James by the arm, pulled him a few feet away from the melee.

"Listen, just so we are clear. You were never here. Guilleme, my officer you see there, will say he struck the Moroccan. It's not a problem. It's better that way for you, for me, for everyone. Don't worry, the Moroccan doesn't know what day it is, let alone what happened."

"OK, Ramon. I don't have a problem either way. I don't mind saying I stopped him, you know."

"Yes I know, James but to be honest... it is my boss. I promised him I would keep you away today. I think from the Daly incident he has got the wrong impression that you are like a vigilante or something. He has a name for you. What was it... oh yes: 'The Equalizer.' So, you would do me a big favour..."

"Fair point, well made," said James, putting on an attempted southern Irish accent. "I'd better disappear then. Let me know what's what, when the dust settles."

"You know it amigo. Take care, oh and James, thanks," said Ramon, nodding with sincerity.

James returned to his moped and revved the accelerator and rode at a more sedate, contemplative pace towards Fornalutx. It had been a good day. In police parlance, they had got a result.

The following day, James was on school run duties to Palma but after dropping Adam and the two girls off at school, he decided to drive into central Palma, parking in the cavernous underground car park along Paseo Maritimo, the main thoroughfare that runs along the seafront of the city from the glorious La Seu Catedral, to the shopping centre at Porto Pi.

He surfaced at the start of his favourite street, Passeig des Born; a wide, Parisian-style boulevard, with glorious, period, seven and eight storey houses, mostly converted into stylish apartments with designer shops or restaurants at street level. In the middle, running almost the full length of the street, was a wide promenade, shaded by mature plane trees, with benches for the weary traveller and a few cafes, where you could sit and watch life in the busy city pass you by.

He took a seat at one of these cafes and ordered fresh orange juice, coffee and a croissant. It had just gone nine and it was a glorious autumnal day and the clear sky was azure blue. He was shaded by the tall buildings, so was glad he had put a jacket on. One thing he had noted about the people of Palma, was just how stylish they were. They always appeared to be well groomed and had a great sense of style for the most part. He reckoned they could probably give Parisians or the Milanese a run for their money on the style front.

He passed an hour sipping his drinks and watching the start of another working day in the capital city. He enjoyed Palma at this time of year, when it reverted mostly to residents and a few astute travellers, who could enjoy Palma and its environs without the masses of tourists who descended on the island during the summer months. Life was a little more sedate and less hectic but with a population of about 400,000, this compact, little city punched above its weight in terms of location, accessibility, culture, history, architecture and gastronomy.

Today, James was there for another of its assets; namely its shops and one in particular: Rialto Living. This, to him, was 'The Mothership'. It was an interior design store like no other. It was previously a baroque-style 'palacio' which, during the eighteenth century had been the home of an Irish military doctor, John O'Ryan and the building had suitably been called Ca'n O'Ryan. In later years, it had been The Rialto Cinema but more recently, it had been converted sympathetically into the most glorious concept store featuring fashion, interiors and a café, by the Swedish owners.

James was on a mission. He would spend some time taking inspiration from the stunningly restored period details of the building's interior and top up his order of Farrow and Ball paint but he was searching for a statement piece for the entrada of his hotel. He had previously had an enormous wrought iron candelabra, covered with copious amounts of molten wax, which had look stunning at night time, fully lit. However, this had been a bespoke piece, made by a local craftsperson for Hotel Artesa and as part of the Hotel's philosophy of being a showcase for local talent, James had decided that all the artwork was for sale to his guests and it was such, that one guest loved it so much, that he bought it and had it shipped home. Unfortunately, the local artist was now working on several commissions in another medium and it would be several months before a replacement could be produced. In the interim period, James required a statement piece that would provide a similar wow factor for the new season opening in February.

As soon as he entered the gallery space of the store, which showcased up and coming local artists, he knew he had found his special piece, for staring at him, as he climbed the stairs, in all its glory, was a most beautiful old photograph, lovingly restored and blown up on canvas by local photographer Miquel Salom. It was a view of Palma cathedral and the adjacent Royal Palace. He made the purchase, eager to hang his new acquisition in its new home and made his way back to his car and then back to the hotel in Fornalutx.

Having completed his mission and more than satisfied with the end result, James' thoughts turned back to the events of the previous day and he decided to give Ramon a ring, to check up on the progress of the interviews and the robbery investigation as a whole.

"Hey Ramon, is it a good time?" asked James.

"It's fine James. We are going to charge them soon. They are admitting the robberies: all three. In fact, they told us of another one, where they didn't get any money or so they said but the victim did not report it to the local police. However, finding the money is a different story. We did a full search of their flat and the scooter and we only found a few €100 notes in their wallets. They are not telling us where the rest of the money is. The combined total from the three successful robberies comes to over €110,000. They know they will get a bigger prison sentence if they don't cooperate but that doesn't seem to worry them. It's very frustrating. We are glad to have caught them but that's not much good to the victims, if we cannot recover most of their stolen money."

"Oh, that is annoying. I was hoping to have good news for my ex-guests from Rutland. Shit! Can you divulge to me what exactly was found during the search of the flat and of them at the Police station?" asked James.

"I don't mind. Two brains are better than one but there is nothing unusual. Hang on, let me get a copy of the search log... right, OK, let's see... various items of clothing, a laptop computer, which is being examined, a pair of binoculars, some white powder believed to be cocaine... mobile phones... nothing out of the ordinary. Nothing to suggest they had a vehicle other than the Vespa and nothing to indicate access to another property."

"What did they have on them when they were arrested?" asked James.

"The usual, wallets, which did however, contain €100 notes, which we know where the denomination of notes given out by the banks for the house sales but we can't prove this... watches, mobiles, house keys, cigarettes, lighters... the usual."

"Let me think about this. You have just done three robberies and you have a lot of cash. You are living close to the scene of the crimes and you don't want to keep the incriminating evidence at your property. You can't just dig a hole and bury it, because you don't have any land at your flat and perhaps you need the money to live off, so you need easy access to it regularly, without raising suspicion but in a place where it is reasonably secure. Wait a minute... Ramon, were there any other keys found, other than house keys, either at the flat or on the Chilean?" asked James.

"Let me check... custody record 2... one key fob containing one Yale-type key and one small key. That was on the Chilean."

"Right," said James excitedly, "This is just a hunch but I think it's worth a punt. When I go to the gym at Son Angelats, I use the lockers outside the gym on the landing and I'm a creature of habit. I almost always use locker four. It's straight in front, as you come up the stairs, at a good height to put your gear in. When I come up the stairs, I look at the lockers and the locked ones without the keys, will be a good indicator of how many people are in the gym…"

"This is all very interesting, James but what has this got to do with the money?"

"I'm just getting to that. I have noticed the Chilean use one of the first two lockers, either one or two. Now recently, a couple of mornings over the last couple of weeks, I have been the first one into the gym but yet, I have expected to see someone else, as another locker is locked and missing its key. It is either locker one or two, I can't remember. Now, I thought nothing of it, as I thought it might be the gym supervisor's locker or something. But now… yes… that would make sense. The guy has access to it from 8am to 10pm at night, six days a week. He keeps the key. No one is any the wiser. It is not as if someone is checking the lockers every day. There is nothing to connect him to it and it is pretty secure but more importantly, accessible without raising suspicion. He could just keep the money in a sports bag and lift out what he and his mate needed for the week. Their very own cash machine. Yes, that's it!" exclaimed James.

"Alright James, it seems plausible enough. I will meet you there in say, one hour?" said Martinez.

"That's fine by me. I want to be there to see if my locker theory is right. Large amounts of cash and lockers and me have a bit of history Ramon," laughed James.

"What do you mean?" asked Ramon, sounding confused.

"Oh nothing," said James quickly, realising that he had almost let the cat out of the bag, regarding his previous undisclosed find of Daly's hoard. "See you there," he added.

James got to the gym before Ramon, eager to at least verify if either locker was still occupied. Both lockers had their keys missing and were locked, so he used his entry pass and entered the gym. There was only one man in the gym. James asked if he was using a locker and was informed he was using locker two. On returning to the foyer area outside the gym, James could see Martinez had arrived and was ascending the stairs towards him.

"I hope this is not a wasted journey for you," said James.

"Don't worry. Even if it is a dead end, I like the way you think. Anyway, it gets me out of the office for a while. Right, here we go," said Ramon, as he reached into his pocket and removed a small key from it. It was devoid of the usual plastic fob that accompanied the other locker keys but James contented himself, that the Chilean had probably discarded it, in case of it being identified in just such a situation as this.

Martinez held the key up to locker two.

"No, I think it is number one," said James.

Martinez placed the key in the lock of locker one. It fitted snugly. He turned the key clockwise and both men heard a click, as the mechanism turned and released a €1 coin. Martinez opened the locker, to reveal it contained a small black sports bag. He lifted the bag from the locker and nodded, as if to acknowledge that the bag had some weight to it. He set it down on a plastic chair at the end of the line of lockers and undid the zip. He reached in and produced a large wad of new €100 bills. Returning them to the bag and scrutinising the contents from within, he turned to James and said,

"I think most of it is there. You are unbelievable! How do you do it? Is it local knowledge that I am missing here, or do you just have a gift for this type of work?" asked Martinez, grinning from ear to ear and shaking his head. "You know my boss is going to be very pleased and this time he is going to be told that you were here. This is a big deal here James. He is going to want to meet you now. Look, I'm going to get this back to the station for safekeeping. This will tie any loose ends together and make the evidence much stronger. I will inform my boss and then I will inform the victims once we count it all. Good work my friend. I will ring you later," said Martinez, as he shook James by the hand, before descending the staircase.

James took a moment, just to wallow in the praise he had just received and it immediately brought to mind his previous find several months before, of the booty he had discovered at Palma airport of Daly's stash. This quickly wiped the self-congratulatory smile from his face, at the realisation that he had kept this knowledge from Martinez. His guilt was halted, as the gym user came from the gym, to access the adjacent locker and James turned and walked down the stairs, uncomfortable in the knowledge that he must continue to conceal his secret for the good of his friend, Matt and himself, if he was to continue to have the friendship and trust of Martinez.

Chapter 8

A Touch of the White Stuff

A sense of normality had returned to James' life, in the weeks leading up to their first Christmas in Mallorca. He had spent a pleasant evening with Inspector Martinez in early December, who along with his boss, Superintendent Jaumo Busquets, had taken him out for a meal at a restaurant in Palma, to thank him for his work in helping them catch the two Soller robbers and in recovering almost all of the victims' money. During the meal, James felt slightly uncomfortable, when Martinez raised his glass and made a toast to James and then informed him that he had put his name forward, for The Medal of Merit for Civil Defence, an honour given for outstanding service by members of the public for exceptional civic duty. James felt that what he had done was not worthy of anything, other than the meal he was receiving and felt less worthy, knowing that he had withheld some information regarding the Daly case, so any future public display of thanks to him, as surely there must be, if it involved the bestowing on him of a medal, did not sit well with him.

He was now in full Christmas mode and had put up a large Christmas tree in the entrada of their house and a holly wreath adorned their front door. The village plaça looked festive, with illuminated signs saying 'Bones Festes' and 'Bon Nadal', meaning Happy Christmas in Calalan, giving the cool evenings a warm glow. Belens or nativity scene models, had been placed in some shop windows and in the homes of the village. Christmas in Mallorca had been taking on more significance in the previous ten years that James had been visiting the island. The most important date in the Spanish Christmas period was still the celebration of Epiphany on 6 January, when Christians believe that Los Tres Reyes Magos or The Three Kings, met the baby Jesus and presented him with their gifts of gold, frankincense and myrrh. It is on this night, rather than on Christmas morning, as in other Northern European countries, that Mallorcan children receive presents. There is no 'Papa Noel' or Santa Claus in sight and presents are handed out by the more important Baltasar, Gaspar and Melchor.

Some northern European influences had been creeping into Mallorca, with an ever-growing number of the islands residents hailing from Germany, Britain and Sweden, amongst others. Christmas trees were now readily available in most of the large DIY stores, along with Christmas decorations. Fresh turkey was available for a traditional Christmas dinner from a British butcher or a frozen alternative, if you wanted it. Christmas Eve or La Nocha Buena, was usually celebrated more than Christmas Day by Mallorcans, who would gather with family members and celebrate together with an evening meal, perhaps of roast lamb.

This would be James' family's first Christmas and New Year on the island and they planned to spend it with some family, who would be visiting and with some friends who lived locally. James had been avoiding Matt since he had been beaten up and had Kusemi's money stolen. He was finding it difficult to conjure up forgiveness, despite the Season of Goodwill being in full swing and was reticent to invite Matt and his family to his house over the festive period. Charlotte had cornered him on a couple of occasions, as to when they would see the Smith family, but James had managed to change the subject. He was still somewhat reluctant to wipe Matt's slate clean, given the high stakes that had been involved, especially regarding James' family being put at risk, although he was still resolute in his promise of non-discloser about Matt.

Over the Christmas period, the Gordon family enjoyed a few outings, mixing their new found Mallorcan culture with their northern European roots. They enjoyed a traditional Christmas market at Poblo Espanyol in Palma, which had a heavy German influence, sampling gluehwein, stollen and gingerbread lebkuchen. Traditional Christmas carols being sung brought back memories of Christmas' past in The UK, as did the annual pilgrimage to a local expat production in Palma of *A Christmas Carol.*

They still adhered to their tradition of Santa Claus leaving presents for Adam and Reuben on Christmas morning. Their boys were still young enough to enjoy the myth surrounding Saint Nicholas but James drew the line at leaving milk, mince pies and a carrot out, something that Charlotte did, regardless. Christmas Day celebrations continued, with a late afternoon Christmas dinner in the large entrada of Hotel Artisan. James' sisters and family and Charlottes' father had come over for Christmas and were being put up in the fine surroundings of the hotel's suites. Some of the guests had attended the Christmas Day service at the Anglican Church of St Philip and St James in Palma. James, however, had spent the morning slaving over his oven, preparing roast lamb and stuffing with lots of trimmings for sixteen.

Family and friends came and went over Christmas and The New Year and James, Charlotte and the two boys celebrated New Year's Eve in Fornalutx plaça, in the traditional Mallorcan way, by eating a grape after each of the twelve strikes of the church clock at midnight. Known as the twelve grapes of luck, it was another local custom they were happy to embrace. The boys seemed more enamoured with the thick, sweet, hot chocolate and 'churros' that were also on offer.

Despite being dry over the period, the temperature had been dropping, so much so, that the weather forecast was showing a 50% chance of snow falling over the following few days. The peaks of The Serra de Tramuntana, had already had a dusting of snow, like some giant cakes, with sieved icing sugar atop. James, Charlotte and the two boys had driven up towards The Blue Gorge for a walk, only to find that the road had been closed by local police, as it was impassable. They then joined many other locals, who appeared mesmerised by the sight of a small covering of 'the white stuff' and who, almost without exception, followed a local custom of building a mini snowman and then placed it on the bonnet of their car, as a trophy to their expedition into the mountains and then they drove back into The Valley and beyond.

Epiphany saw the village all-abuzz, with the council workers getting the stage ready for the evenings' main event. The Mayor was there to oversee the preparations. Rows of chairs filled the small square to its full capacity. Darkness had descended on the village but the antique-style streetlights and the additional Christmas lights gave the intimate streets a warm, amber glow. The bars were busy and additional tables had been set out, for what was one of the biggest events in the villages' social calendar.

An icy wind blew in from the North and James thought he could detect a few wispy snowflakes rising and falling on the breeze. The crowds were now lining the streets in expectation of three important dignitaries and their visit to the village. James lifted Reuben up onto his shoulders to get a better view. He could hear the clip clop of horses' hooves and peered over the hoard to see The Three Kings, in all their fine costumes, sitting on top of their large horses. They dispensed handfuls of sweets to the appreciative children, who lined their route. They then, with a degree of horsemanship and dexterity mounted the wide steps up to the church, where a short service took place and then the Magi took a seat on their three thrones on the stage in the plaça, for the eagerly awaited present giving ceremony.

Both Adam and Reuben had written letters to The Three Kings on Boxing Day and handed them into 'The Adjuntament' or council office for onward delivery. James watched, with a warming glass of mulled wine in hand, as all the local children were called up on stage, by name, one at a time, to have bestowed on them presents from the three gift givers. Rather than spoil the two boys, James and Charlotte limited their presents to three each, their boys having already benefitted from those received from Papa Noel on Christmas morning. The atmosphere was warm and jovial. The alcoholic beverages were helping to enhance the ambiance too. The crowd was made up mostly of local and expat residents but there were a few guests from the Ca'n Reus Hotel, which was one of the hardy breed of small hotels in the area, which remained open over the festive season. James took comfort in the knowledge that he too would play host to paying guests in Hotel Artesa the following year and that they would be rewarded with such a pleasant, traditional spectacle.

His thoughts were interrupted by the announcement, that it was Reuben Gordon's turn and James watched the face of his son change, from one of initial apprehension at having to sit on the lap of a 'blacked up' male, whilst replying to his questions in Catalan, to one of sheer delight, when presented with three wrapped gifts. The delight was slightly more subdued on the face of his older son Adam, when eventually it became his turn.

Children played with their newly acquired possessions, whilst parents drank and chatted. James watched the faces of all in attendance. He felt a great sense of solidarity with these people, who, he thought, should not be pigeonholed as Mallorcan or British or German but rather as people of the human race. He was one of the fortunate few, who had stumbled upon this special little village many years previously and it was at times like this, that made him realise what a special place The Soller Valley was and for the most part, just how generous in spirit, the native locals were. As he basked in the warmth of his thoughts and in the large measure of Mallorcan brandy he had been given, the snow began to fall.

Chapter 9

More White Stuff

The temperate, winter months soon morphed into spring and with the increase in temperature and longer days, came a new tourist season. For James and Hotel Artesa, the season was already well under way, having re-opened the doors at the end of February. The hotel had played host to an array of cycling aficionados and walking fanatics throughout March and April. Lovers of nature, had arrived from late February, to capture the aromatic and colourful display of almond blossom that filled the trees, until the wind and Mother Nature jettisoned their adornments to the ground, like a carpet of wedding confetti. The celebrations of Lent and Easter had proven to be as uplifting and as colourful as he had witnessed, whilst on holiday in previous years. During Easter week, or Semana Santa, James had gone to Soller with his family, to experience the differing moods of the processions. From the solemn, silent and macabre procession of the penitents, dressed in coloured, pointed hats akin to the Ku Klux Klan, on

Dijous Sant, or Maundy Thursday, to the more upbeat and celebratory overtones on Easter Sunday, celebrating the Resurrection.

Hotel Artesa had been full, throughout the Easter celebrations, with 100% occupancy levels. James had been working religiously on the hotel's new website and was now seeing the rewards for his diligence. He was now achieving over 50% of their bookings directly through this. The remainder, they were getting through the various on-line holiday booking websites, where they had the privilege of paying them 30% commission. James felt this commission was a little excessive but this was the nature of the beast and he had gone into the business, knowing the charges involved.

Towards the end of April, he received a two night, last minute booking. He had had a last minute cancellation, so the guest was fortunate to find the last, remaining room was vacant for their required dates. The booking had come via one of the on-line companies and was the first single-occupancy booking he had taken since the hotel opened. They tended to get, almost exclusively couples, although, they did have a family suite, accommodating four people.

Since the opening of the hotel, over six months previously, James had found that over 30% of the clientele his hotel was attracting, were gay couples and primarily gay men. Neither Charlotte nor he had a problem with this, as perhaps some of their former countryman might have had and for them, 'The Pink Pound' was proving to be a very lucrative part of their income stream. In fact, if anything, James took it as a complement, that his hotel was proving to be so attractive to this section of society, who appeared, to him, to have discerning taste in art and interior design. When he had remarked to his friend, Paul, on this phenomenon, he simply replied, 'Fifty Shades of Grey', which had become his nickname for James, due to his love for various shades of Farrow and Ball paint from the grey pallet, which he used in the décor of Hotel Artesa.

His new guest arrived and was welcomed. She was a relatively young guest by the early standards of the hotel, at about 25 years old, he guessed. She was travelling on a Lithuanian passport and was not quite what he had expected. She had just one piece of luggage, namely hand luggage, in the form of a grey, rigid Samsonite case.

"Welcome to Hotel Artesa. I hope you had a pleasant journey. My name is James and if I, or indeed any other member of staff can do anything to improve your stay here, don't hesitate to ask. Now, if I can just take details of a credit card and I need to take a copy of your passport. There is an 'honesty bar' in the corner, behind you, with an extensive range of drinks and also there is a small fridge in your room with some complementary soft drinks. Over here to the left, you will find magazines and daily newspapers. Breakfast is served between eight and ten and usually on the terrace, weather permitting. Have you been to Fornalutx before?" asked James.

"No. This is first time," said the girl, with a strong accent.

"How did you come to hear about us?

"I have friend who will visit and lives nearby," said the girl, clearly trying to find the right words in English.

James handed her the key to her room and then walked round from behind the reception desk and placing his hand on her case said,

"Let me take this up for you."

"No! It is OK. I carry case," she said abruptly and then seemingly realising her brusqueness, added, "The handle is weak, sorry."

James was a little taken aback but put it down to her character and nationality. He had been smiling at her, in an effort to make her feel welcome but there had been no sign of her cracking a smile back. Indeed, she was somewhat stoical in her demeanour. He led the way to her second floor suite, opened the door for her and bid her a pleasant stay.

He then returned to his position, behind the reception desk and continued with his duties. A couple of hours later, he heard the front door of the hotel open, and in walked a man, in his late forties, carrying a small, grey Samsonite hand luggage case, that looked identical to the one carried by his new Lithuanian guest, apart from this one having a small but noticeable dent on the front panel. He approached the reception desk.

"Hola. Que tal?" came the greeting.

"Moy bien. Digame," replied James.

As he looked at the man, he realised that he had seen him somewhere before but he couldn't remember where.

The man was looking at James now in half-recognition and he then nodded, seeming to realise where he had seen him before.

"You are friend of Kiwi?" the man asked, in English.

The mention of the name, Kiwi, immediately made the penny drop for James. Kiwi, aptly named, was a friend of James', originally from New Zealand who, until recently, had lived on the outskirts of Fornalutx, with his wife and young family and had been a tree surgeon and landscape gardener. He had since moved to Dubai for the next couple of years. Kiwi had helped James choose some plants for the courtyard of the hotel, prior to his move and it was the man, standing in front of him, who had sold him the plants, at his garden centre, near Santa Maria.

"Ah yes, I am a friend of Kiwi's. I know you now. Santa Maria garden centre?"

"Si, si, si. I am here to see my friend, Emilija," said the man.

Realising he meant his new Lithuanian guest, James replied,

"Sure. She's in room five. Top of the stairs, first door on your right."

"Muchos gracias," he replied, as he made his way to the stairwell and up the stairs.

About half an hour later, the man passed James, who was still behind the reception desk and smiled and waved saying, "Adios." He was wheeling a grey Samsonite case, as on his arrival but James noted that this time, it was devoid of the dent he had noticed, on the one on his way in. He thought this was somewhat peculiar but didn't give it any more thought.

The next morning James and Charlotte served breakfast to their guests. Emilija arrived for breakfast just as they were clearing up at ten o'clock, so James told her to help herself to cereal and asked her if she would like tea or coffee. She finished breakfast about half an hour later and he then saw her leave the hotel shortly afterwards, as Charlotte and he were going about their duties.

An hour or so later, Monica came to the reception desk.

"Sorry, James. I thought you should know. I have been cleaning in room five and I noticed quite bad scratches to the top of the antique chest of drawers in the room. Perhaps, you want to have a look?" said Monica.

"I'm sure it's fine but I will take a quick look, as I know the guest is out."

James accompanied Monica to room five. He wouldn't normally go into a guests' room but Monica was still finding her feet and he wanted to see if she was being over-fastidious, or was right to bring it to his attention, especially as the piece of furniture concerned, was a family heirloom. He expected things to take some abuse but he thought there was no harm in appeasing Monica.

They both entered the room and Monica pointed to the top of the chest of drawers, which was an antique mahogany, late Georgian two over three chest of drawers.

"I wouldn't have bothered you, only, the scratches won't disappear, even after I have polished it," said Monica.

James looked at the top and noted numerous, shallow, straight scratches which were much lighter than the darker patina of the old top.

"Yes, I see what you mean. Thanks Monica, I'll sort it out."

Monica left the room, leaving James to look at the scratches. It reminded him of the sort of marks that he had witnessed before in his policing career, when he had been in the Drugs Squad. He had seen similar scratches to furniture made by a razor blade, when used for chopping up illegal substances, usually cocaine.

He was beginning to get suspicious. He opened the wardrobe in the room and found a grey Samsonite case. He checked it and found that it had a dent to its front panel.

'This is the case her friend brought with him', he thought. 'Why swap cases?'

The case was locked but it was fairly light, so it appeared not to have much, if anything, inside. He had a cursory check of the room and noted that the girl had few belongings with her. He then realised that she had been wearing the same clothes at breakfast that she had arrived in. He checked the bathroom and found it contained only a toothbrush but on opening the bathroom cabinet, he saw a small packet of baking soda. Alarm bells started ringing loudly in his head. He could think of no other legitimate reason why someone, who was travelling so lightly, would have baking soda with them, other than to cut it with base cocaine.

He left the room, in case his presence was discovered by the room's occupant and he returned to the reception area. He had seen evidence of drug use on numerous occasions. He felt a degree of sympathy with drug users, who were addicts and he could sympathise with their plight and even some of their criminal actions that arose from them having a need to feed their habit. Who he had no sympathy for though, were those who were engaged in the production, importation and distribution of these controlled drugs. Those involved, were in it for pure profit and would normally go to whatever means were necessary, to protect their criminal enterprises.

James decided to ring his friend Kiwi, in order to find out more information on their mutual acquaintance.

"Hey, mate. How's it going over there?" asked James.

"Yeah, pretty good. It has taken the boys a while to settle into their new schools and it has taken us a while to get used to the heat, but it's only for a while and it's a great experience. How is the hotel business doing?" asked Kiwi.

"It's going well. Listen, I wanted to pick your brains. Do you know the guy who owns the garden centre near Santa Maria; the one I got the plants from, when you were with me?"

"Oh yeah, that'd be Lluc Arbona. I used to get most of my plants from him and occasionally, when I did some landscaping jobs on Ibiza, he would ask me to take over some plants and bags of compost to a mate of his called Alvaro. Why do you ask?"

"How well do you know Lluc?"

"I've only known him for a couple of years. He was always pleasant to me but I did hear a few rumours just as I was leaving to come here," said Kiwi.

"What sort of rumours?"

"Well, just that one or two of my local clients didn't want their plants to come from him, as they said he had got mixed up in drugs or something. To be honest, it was beginning to hurt my business and when I come back, I'll be looking for a new supplier. Of plants, that is!" laughed Kiwi.

"Kiwi, I have to tell you, I think he's been at it, in my hotel. How often did he ask you to take plants and bags of compost to Ibiza?"

"Usually, only when I had jobs lined up, which could be once a month or less. He did ask me to take some stuff over for him, when I didn't have my own work and he paid me for going. You don't think... oh, bloody hell mate! Do you think he was using me, to carry some gear or whatever they call it? The cheeky bastard! You know, I did wonder why he asked me when I wasn't specifically going but I was happy to go, as it was quiet here. I could have been nicked and I wouldn't have known a thing about it and I'd have been classed as a right liar, like all those other gormless drug mules, who plead their innocence but in my case, it would have been true. What are you going to do, mate?" asked Kiwi.

"I don't know yet but I can't stand drug deals going on in my hotel. It's not the sort of establishment I was hoping for. Listen, you take care and I'll see you soon."

"If you do catch the bastard, give him a slap for me, will you? Take care. Bye."

James came off the phone, deep in thought. He was piecing together a clear picture in his head, as to, not only what had happened in his hotel the previous day but what was happening beyond this. He decided to go home and ring Martinez.

"Hey Ramon. Que tal?"

"I'm good, James. And you?" he enquired.

"I'm sorry to be always ringing you with problems or crazy notions but I don't think I can ignore this one. Yesterday, I had a Lithuanian girl check into the hotel by herself, which is unusual. She then, had a visitor, who I had met before. It seemed that they have swapped cases. To cut a long story short, I think she is a drug mule, bringing cocaine into Mallorca and he is her connection here and he called for the gear last night. I found scratches to a chest of drawers in her room and baking soda. I think he arrived, took a small sample of the base cocaine, cut it up on the chest of drawers and mixed in the baking powder and checked the product. His name apparently, is Lluc Arbona."

"Did you say Lluc Arbona? Are you sure?" asked Ramon quickly.

"I was told this by a friend of mine, who used to buy plants from him at his garden centre in Santa Maria, which is where I had seen him before. Why?" asked James.

"Because I had heard from one of my sources, that he has recently become involved in the drugs trade but I didn't believe him, because the gardening business is successful and has been a family run enterprise for over thirty years. Arbona has no previous convictions and I used to play football against him about twenty years ago. I thought my source was wrong. What you have just told me, is making me have a re-think."

"There's more. My friend also told me, that Arbona occasionally asked him to take plants and bags of compost over to Ibiza. My friend is very anti-drugs and a good guy, so if he had been taking drugs over to Ibiza, he definitely didn't know he was doing it. Look Ramon, the girl is young. She's not our usual type of guest and when I offered to carry her case, she nearly had a heart attack. There is definitely something not right here and I certainly don't want this going on in my hotel. What will the neighbours think? Since I am the neighbours, I can tell you: they don't like it and they want to put a stop to it."

"This is enough information for me to be able to search his home and his business. We shouldn't wait. I will need to arrest the girl and search the room she is staying in also. Give me half an hour and I will ring you with a time for the searches. Ciao."

James returned next door to his hotel and awaited Martinez' phone call, during which time, the Lithuanian girl returned to the hotel and was having a late afternoon drink on the terrace. A short time later, his mobile rang.

"My guys will be with you in fifteen minutes James. I am going to Santa Maria. Is the girl there?"

"She's just come back and is having a drink. If she tries to leave, I'll try to keep her here. Good luck."

"We'll speak after, my friend."

Like clockwork, fifteen minutes later, the hotel door opened and in walked two detectives, one of whom, James had briefly met before and the other was a female detective. He pointed to the location of the girl and he accompanied them to the rear courtyard.

The female detective then spoke to James' guest in English and told her that she was being arrested on suspicion of the importation of controlled drugs and she was handcuffed. All four then went to her room at the top of the stairs. A full search of the room was conducted in her presence and the baking soda was seized. She was told to open the lock on the Samsonite case, which she did. Inside was €2,000 in cash and several wraps of cocaine. It was obvious to all concerned, that this was her payment for her role as a drugs mule, probably having flown in from South America, thought James. The officers left with the evidence and their prisoner and he heard them relay the information to Martinez.

James walked the few steps to his home and informed Charlotte of what had happened. She had been concerned that the hotel may receive bad publicity as a result but James assured her, that Martinez would not let that happen.

It was nearly midnight, when James received a call on his mobile phone, which was by his bed. It was Martinez.

"I didn't wake you, did I?" he asked.

"It's OK. I tried to ring you earlier, as I hadn't heard anything but your phone just went to voicemail."

"Yeah, I know. We have only just finished the search here. Unbelievable! We had to go through over 200 bags of compost and over an acre of plants. The drugs dogs didn't pick anything up for the first two hours of the search. Obviously, I had heard the result of the search at your place but I thought, maybe he was smart enough to keep it somewhere other than at his home or his garden centre but then, they started picking up the scent. Wow! That was hard work but worth the effort. We recovered over 10kg of 90% pure cocaine, with an estimated street value of over two million euros. What is it you say, James? That's a result!" said Martinez, laughing.

"Brilliant, Ramon. Well done," said James.

"No, my friend. Well done is what I and my boss say to you. We will be interviewing and charging them both soon. Good work my friend."

James informed a curious Charlotte as to his news and then both rolled over to sleep. It had been a successful day and James was content with the result but this was tempered with a little annoyance, that his hotel had been used as a drugs exchange venue.

The following day, Martinez rang to inform him that neither suspect was saying anything but both would be charged and remanded in custody to Palma prison, awaiting their trial. They had found the other Samsonite case in Arbona's car and it was clear that someone had expertly made secret compartments in the case, which is where the recent batch of the cocaine had been secreted, in vacuum-packed containers, which in turn were covered in fabric softener, in order to attempt to throw the drugs dogs off the scent at the airport.

Chapter 10

Firo

It was now the second week of May. Hotel Artesa was full of guests and James was preparing for the biggest event in the Valley's busy social calendar: The Firo. This fiesta was a re-enactment, celebrating the residents of Sollers' victory over the Moors in 1561 and went on for four days. James had decided to embrace this event, to the point that he had purchased various items of clothing, to help transform himself into a Moorish invader for The Firo on the following Monday, when hundreds of people would be dressed as Sollerics from the 16th century and the opposing Moorish invaders. A sham fight would then take place at two locations in Port de Soller, with some of the invaders arriving by boat, before the first, full-scale battle turned the beach into a cloud of sulphur, emanating from an eruption of gunfire from their blunderbusses. The stage would then move into Soller itself, with more mayhem and finally the crowd would take part in an emotionally-charged rendition of La Balanguera, the Mallorcan national anthem. This was made even more emotional, by the copious amount of alcohol that would be enjoyed by the amicable crowd and was a vehicle for the modern day, indigenous Sollerics, to show a display of unity against the repression suffered under Franco. James saw it also as a way for the locals to, in that moment, show their Mallorcan nationalism in the face of a new era of invaders, namely tourists and expats, but then reverted to type, with the realisation that they and the island were dependent on these 'invaders' or 'Los Guiris'.

The previous day had been Fira, a more family-orientated celebration of local crafts and a Mallorcan version of an agricultural show, with an array of animals being sold. Today was the main event and James was already in costume and had been transformed, with the help of a tin of tan Kiwi shoe polish. He had served breakfast to the early risers in the hotel, much to their amusement and also with a degree of admiration from them, at the lengths he had gone to, as was customary by all who took part in Firo, in search of realism. He, as a Saracen, now sported a turban, a bejewelled waistcoat, spacious pantaloons and an ornate sabre dagger with scabbard, tucked into his waist belt. He was unrecognisable as his former self.

Reuben's school was closed for Firo and he was looking forward to taking part in his first Firo, as a resident of the Valley and a Mallorquin-speaking one at that. He was dressed in a traditional 16th century Mallorcan boy's finery and was to go with Charlotte to meet a couple of his classmates and their mothers. Adam, however, still had school to attend in Palma and did not get a days' holiday, as the fiesta was not an island-wide public holiday, although it was also celebrated later in the year in Pollensa.

Mid-afternoon, James set off on his scooter and made his way to Port de Soller. The main battles would not take place until after five pm. Extra trams had been laid on to convey the participants from Soller to its port and back and as James got close to the Port, he could see several trams full of people. The majority of their occupants were already in costume, with the red and white half crescent Moorish flags and the crusader's flag of St George and both were being draped out of the carriages. James thought one might be forgiven for thinking that the carriages were carrying England and Turkey football fans, heading to a match.

The Policia Local and The Guardia Civil were out in force. It was a day when crowd management was required, to deal with the influx of several thousand additional visitors, mostly Mallorcans, from across the island. In addition, there was a large percentage of the thirteen thousand Valley residents who took part or watched the spectacle. Add to that a good number of inquisitive tourists and you had mayhem, if a degree of crowd management was not exercised.

James had arranged to meet another couple of expat residents. Dave had been living in Soller for 10 years and Jesus was from Valencia but had been a Soller resident for five years. Both had taken part in the festivities several years running and were eager to embrace the culture and continue the wonderful tradition.

The road was busy and people were tooting their car horns and yelling out from their cars, as they passed the throngs of people walking along the footpaths, heading for the Port.

As James approached their meeting point of a bar along the promenade, he could make out Dave and Jesus, dressed in similar Moorish garb to himself. They were sitting at a table with another Saracen and as he arrived and greeted his two friends, he soon realised that the third man, despite being disguised in costume, was none other than Matt.

He had been deliberately avoiding Matt, since his revelation about his early past but more importantly to James, after he revealed the part he had played in the murder of Chas Daly. He had not forgiven him for putting him and his family in harm's way and although, he acknowledged, there had been mitigating circumstances, James had found it hard to rekindle the previous friendship he had once shared with Matt. After greeting his other two friends he turned to Matt and said quietly,

"Well, this is a bit awkward."

"I know, I know. I'm sorry," said Matt, apologetically.

"Alright. Well we're both here now, so let's not let it spoil everyone else' day. Fair enough?" asked James.

"No problem with me. I don't have a problem with you. I just wish you could say the same about me," said Matt, raising his eyebrows.

James frowned and shook his head, to indicate he didn't want the subject discussed any further.

"Right. Who needs another drink?" asked James, standing up.

"Do you really need an answer to that question?" said Jesus, smiling.

"Nope. Four beers it is then," said James, making his way to the crowded bar.

He returned a short time later with the drinks. Matt leaned over to James, as he sat down beside him.

"I need to speak to you in private, when we get a minute though. I need to tell you something."

James looked at Matt directly, after receiving this ominous revelation and said,

"OK. Well, there's no time like the present."

He returned to his feet and motioned with his head for Matt to follow him. Both men walked a few feet out of the bar but the noise from the passing groups of revellers, who were intermittently discharging their shotguns with blank cartridges, made it very difficult to hear.

"I needed to speak to you," started Matt, putting his fingers in his ears. "I got a phone call last night from Danny. It appears, he has got word that his guy Kingpin, has stopped paying the Russians and they are pissed off. They have said that all bets are off. He rang in a bit of a state. He thinks they are going to top him. He also told me to warn you, as he thinks that they still harbour some resentment towards you."

"Oh great!" said James, shaking his head. "Do you understand now, why I might still be a bit pissed off with you Matt?"

"Mate, I know. I'm really sorry about this. Perhaps you should tell your mate Martinez about this latest development."

"I will, but I didn't bring my mobile with me. Have you got yours?" asked James.

"No. Sorry. I have no pockets big enough in this outfit. Look, I'm sure it will keep until later. Try and not let this spoil your day," said Matt, placing his hand on James' shoulder.

"Alright. I'll ring him later," said James, sighing.

They both returned to their table and after several more beers, the four made their way to the first battle site on the beach. The noise was deafening, as hundreds of participants in costume descended on the beach, discharging blank rounds, fireworks and firecrackers. There was a cloud of smoke all around them and visibility was restricted to a few metres.

Suddenly Matt, who was walking beside James, shouted something towards him. It was too noisy for him to discern what he had said. James then felt Matt leap on top of him and both men fell to the ground. Thinking Matt had taken his acting part to extremes, James was not amused. Matt was still lying face down on the sand, as he picked himself up.

"Get up, you silly bugger. What was that for?" he asked, giving Matt a gentle prod with his foot.

Matt still didn't move and he was now in danger of being trampled by the on-coming crowd making ready for the mock battle. James kneeled down over him, concerned for both their welfare. He turned Matt over to reveal a large, wet, dark patch to Matt's chest. It became immediately evident to James, that he had been shot. James had not realised, since the number of weapons being discharged had reached fever pitch. This had been a live round. This was no accident. Suddenly panic engulfed him. He realised that Matt had obviously seen someone in front of them and had then thrown himself in front of James, to protect him. He had quite literally taken a bullet for him. Judging from the amount of blood coming from a chest wound, he thought that the bullet may have hit his vital organs and although Matt was still alive, without medical assistance quickly, any hope of survival was diminishing by the second.

Disregarding the potential danger that the shooter may still be present, he got to his feet and yelled at Jesus and Dave, both of whom turned and made their way back the few feet to him.

"Quickly! Matt's been shot!" he yelled, as both men looked down at the sand in disbelief.

"Help me lift him back to the promenade!" demanded James of his friends.

All three men bent down and quickly carried Matt off the beach and laid him onto the pavement. Jesus shouted in the direction of two paramedics, who were on duty close by and James told Dave to get the Guardia Civil as quickly as possible. Two paramedics quickly arrived and set about performing CPR on Matt. A crowd had quickly gathered around them and several Guardia Civil officers arrived, to keep them back. James approached one of them and asked if he spoke English. This was no time for him to try and formulate broken sentences in Spanish. To James' relief the officer nodded.

"I need you to contact Inspector Ramon Martinez from the National Crime Branch in Palma. This man has been shot. I think I was the target. If I'm right, the gunman is a Bosnian hitman, working for the Russian mafia, based in London. Martinez will give you all his details but for now, I can tell you, he is about 1.85m in height, stocky build, with dark hair, slicked back from his forehead. I didn't see him shoot but it has to have been him."

James watched, as the officer relayed the information on his police radio and then produced a mobile phone, as he received an incoming call. He could tell it was Martinez, who was now giving the officer further details of the suspect. The officer then passed the phone to James.

"James, it is Ramon. Listen my friend; you need to get out of there. It is not safe for you. Where are Charlotte and the boys?" asked Martinez.

"Charlotte and Reuben are here somewhere and Adam will back from school by now. Why?"

"It's just a precaution. I don't think the Russians would target your wife or kids but we can't take any risks. I have been trying to ring you since about two o'clock today and I have left messages on your phone. Danny Kusemi was killed last night in prison. He had his throat cut. I wasn't told until I came on duty at two pm. I have spoken to DS Wiggins in London and he had heard that Kusemi's gang had stopped paying the Russians money and he thinks that is why Kusemi was killed."

"Listen, Ramon, I have got to go. I need to try and find Charlotte and Reuben. In the meantime, could you send a couple of officers to my house, just until I get back?"

"Of course. You go with the Guardia Civil officer and let me speak to him again," said Martinez.

James returned the mobile phone to the Guardia Civil officer. He watched as Martinez was briefing him further over the phone. The officer then turned to James and said,

"You must stay with me and we will find your wife and son together."

The officer called to a colleague, who then joined them. James was still watching the paramedics working on Matt. They had placed him on a stretcher but at least, it appeared that he was breathing, if not conscious. They wheeled him towards their ambulance and placed him inside and then quickly drove off through the large crowd with sirens blaring. James turned towards the next task in hand. He asked for the officer's mobile and rang Charlottes' mobile. Surprised at her being able to hear her phone ring, he was taken aback when she answered.

"Oh, Charlotte, good. Where are you?" bellowed James.

"I'm at Don Pedro's having a coffee. Why?" replied Charlotte.

"Wait there. Do not move and make sure Reuben stays with you. I'm coming to get you."

"James, what's wrong? You're scaring me, the way you scared me before. Has that raised its head again? Please, tell me if something has happened?" asked a clearly distressed Charlotte.

"It's just a precaution. I'll be there in five minutes."

James hung up before he had to answer any more awkward questions and so as to get to her with the police as quickly as possible. He relayed her whereabouts to the officer, who ushered him into a waiting car and they set off with 'blues and two's' going and arrived at Don Pedro's restaurant at the Repic end of the beach. Charlotte was waiting with Reuben.

"Get in and I'll explain," said James, helping them both into the car, before telling the officers to make for Fornalutx. He then recounted the earlier incident to Charlotte, who put her arm round Reuben, in a protective manner and she was silent for the duration of the journey, clearly shaken by what she had been told.

Once in Fornalutx, the Guardia Civil officers accompanied the family home. They found that Adam was already in the company of two of Martinez' men. The Guardia Civil officers left them in their protective custody and told James that they would get him word as to Matt's condition. James then realised that no one had contacted Jayne, Matt's wife. He then made the difficult call, informing her of what had happened and told her to make her way to the hospital at Son Espases.

He then turned to Charlotte.

"You three can't stay here. I am a target and by you staying here, I am making you targets. I want you to go back to N. Ireland for a little while, until this blows over. Stay with your Dad."

"We can't just leave. The boys have school for another few weeks. It is important, especially for Adam," said Charlotte, in an exasperated tone.

"OK. OK. Look, if it helps, I'm sorry. What happened here today has had nothing to do with me. Listen, why don't you go and stay with Steven and Sarah in Calvia. I'm sure they would put you up for a few days, under the circumstances. I will have a word with Ramon and I'm sure he will put a couple of officers on guard duty, to keep an eye out."

"I don't have much choice, do I? I am not letting Adam miss school. Reuben can have a few more days off. He's not the issue. Where are you going to go?" asked Charlotte.

"I'm not going anywhere. I have a business to run. I can't just leave guests to their own devices and Monica couldn't cope on her own. There is no way they would try and shoot me now. Please, Charlotte, it is one less thing for me to worry about, if I know you guys are safe," pleaded James.

"OK. We'll go and stay at Sarah's."

A short time later, Charlotte returned to the living room, to confirm their plans and that one of Martinez' men would drive them. They left as soon as darkness fell, leaving James alone with his thoughts, apart from a guard in his entrada.

'Deja vu,' he thought, at the realisation that once again, he had a police guard in his house.

'It didn't end terribly well for the guard on that occasion', he thought.

He had been running over the events of that day and over the information that had been disclosed to him. He realised that this would probably be the straw to break the camel's back, as far as Charlotte was concerned. He couldn't see her wanting to remain on the island, after yet another murder attempt on his life. That was what had just happened. He was struggling to comprehend the enormity of the situation. Within a period of about nine months, he had had two attempts made on his life. He was incredulous to this fact.

He had been in dangerous circumstances during the twelve years he had been in the Police in London and Belfast. He had been petrol bombed in Belfast and in riot situations and had been shot at in London whilst giving chase to armed robbery suspects, but at no time had he been individually and specifically targeted, with the singular motive of being killed. He started to go through the motions in his head, of how he would market his new hotel and house. It could take a while for them to sell. He had some savings but without staying to run the hotel, these would quickly be eroded.

Frustrated by the very real prospects he was now facing, he rang Martinez.

"Ramon, it's me. Any news?" he asked.

"Your friend has come out of surgery. He is still critical but the operation was successful, in as far as they were able to stem the blood and repair the damage to his vital organs. The doctors think he will make it but at a cost. The bullet hit his spinal cord and they are not sure if he will ever walk again," said Martinez.

James arranged with Martinez for a guard to be sent to Calvia. Martinez told him that details of Ale Boris had been circulated Europe-wide, for attempted murder. They both realised, that he had been able to get back into Mallorca undetected, despite being wanted for the incident with the bullet, so James had no great faith in him being picked up any time soon.

Over the next few days, he continued running his hotel, as normally as he could, under the circumstances. He tried to keep up a front, as he didn't want his depressed mood to spoil the stay of any of his guests. He did, however, feel it prudent to stay either in his hotel or within the confines of his home, sending Monica to the shops for their daily provisions. He was in contact with Charlotte by phone daily and he had been informed that Matt was making steady progress and was now out of danger, although a full recovery was still in doubt. James had sent Matt a card and some flowers with a message, simply saying,

'Thank-you. You saved my life. I will always be in your debt. Your friend, James.'

He felt cooped up. His life had changed irrevocably. His family were lodging with friends, away from him. He couldn't go about his daily life the way he had been doing. He had been advised not to go anywhere that was not absolutely essential. That meant no trips to the gym, the beach, a bar, no visiting friends and even a trip to the village shop was inadvisable, in case Ale Boris tried to take a pot shot at him again.

'Was this going to continue until they either got Ale Boris, or he was successful in shooting him?' thought James. He had to try to change this situation, before he went mad. He rang Martinez to voice his frustrations.

"Ramon, I don't know how long I can continue like this. I am away from my family and I can't go out. I am confined to the house and I feel like I'm just waiting for the axe to fall. I have to do something!" cried James, with exasperation. "I have been thinking. What if Ale Boris hasn't gone home? What if he's simply waiting for another opportunity? He can't go back to his boss and say, 'Sorry boss, I missed' and expect for things to be fine. No, if I know his type, he won't be happy until he completes his mission, that is: me in a box. So, this is what I have decided. This is my decision and I'm going to do it, whether you like it or not. I am going to start going on my runs again. If he is watching out for me, then it will bring him out in the open. He will see it as his chance to finish the job. All I ask is that you give me a few days to see if he is around and to give me some additional back up for the duration of my runs; an hour at most in the evening. What do you say Ramon? Can I count on your support?"

"Support? Yes, you can count on that. But James, that would be sending you out with a target on your back. My boss would never allow it."

"He doesn't have to know. Please Ramon, I need to do this. I can't live like this any longer," pleaded James.

"I must be mad even considering such a thing... OK, but you do things exactly as I say, understood?" said Martinez, forcefully.

"Understood," agreed James.

"I will allow you to go running for half an hour for three nights. It might take him a while to notice you and to implement things. This is, of course in the unlikely event, he is still around. I believe he is back in the UK, but I will do this for you. You will wear light body armour under your running gear. It will only protect you from low calibre bullets. If he decides to take a head... well, you know the risks, James. I will come myself with three other officers and be in place and watch you, as you run. You will be 'mic'd up' and we will be in permanent contact throughout. OK, we will start tomorrow night."

James felt relieved, that he was now going to be able to try and flush out Ale Boris, if he was still there. His frustration dissipated in the knowledge that he could once again be the master of his own destiny, despite acknowledging the risks involved.

The following day was just a blur to him. He could not focus on anything other than getting out on his planned run. He had several lots of guests leaving that morning and new ones arriving in the afternoon. Monica had been a godsend. She had taken on extra hours of work, despite having school-age children of her own but had arranged that her husband would look after their kids in the interim period, allowing her to assist James, until hopefully Charlotte could return. Jayne had kindly offered to help out but James knew that she had her three boys to look after and she was visiting Matt daily in hospital, so had her hands full.

Monica and he were coping but he hoped that he could put an end to this whole situation, which was proving untenable for him.

Martinez arrived at the hotel, posing as a guest, in case Ale Boris had the hotel under surveillance. In his suitcase, he had brought with him, Kevlar light body armour and the necessary communication equipment. James got ready, whilst Martinez joined his three colleagues at two observation points, along the course of where he was to run. Other uniform personnel had been put on stand-by and were close by, if required. James had to take a pre-designated route and the run should take no more than half an hour.

He took a deep breath and checked that the sound quality in his microphone was satisfactory and so too his receiving sound earpiece, disguised as head-phones. Both were in order. He set off to the sound of Martinez wishing him good luck. He had dispensed with his usual iPod for company but had not relinquished his even more necessary equipment; his pre-scription sunglasses. He wanted to be able to make out any potential sighting of Boris from a distance, which, without his sunglasses, would make everything in the distance, simply a blur.

He took one of his usual running routes, heading out of the village to the north. The road took him uphill on a fairly steep ascent and James found the going harder than usual. He put this down to his lack of running the previous week and also due to the stressful situation he had put himself in. He had effectively made himself a sacrificial lamb. He continued, panting and puffing in the late evening sun. He was giving as few words of commentary as possible. He knew he had at least two sets of eyes on him and three, if Ale Boris was in town and looking in on their little charade.

He continued to the top of the road, until he came to the T-junction with the main road, known locally as 'The American Road'. He had been extra vigilant the whole way and had only been passed by a couple of rental cars and a local villager on a moped. He turned and made his way back down the hill, in the direction of the village. He could hear the sound of something behind him. He turned to see two cyclists approaching him, free-wheeling downhill. They rode past him without incident. He continued through the village and slowly climbed up the steps of the plaça and walked with his hands on his hips, along his street and opened the door of his house. His guard inside was there to meet him and gave him a thumbs up sign.

James' emotions were mixed. On the one hand, he was glad to have returned home in one piece but on the other hand, he was annoyed that he hadn't, if not directly been shot at, at least, heard a radio communication that indicated, that they had located Boris. He consoled himself with the fact that, even if he was being watched, that it could take Ale Boris a day or two to seize his opportunity; to satisfy himself that it wasn't a trap.

Martinez debriefed him over the radio and stated there had been no suspicious sightings throughout the duration of the operation. James would run again the following evening. He took a shower and turned in early for the night, still disappointed at no obvious sign of a resolution.

He continued with his normal routine, the following day and served breakfast to his guests and remained in the hotel until five pm, before returning next door to his home. He then set off for his run at eight pm and took the same route again. His legs were a little stiff after the previous night's run and the fact that he hadn't done any stretching. It proved to be a little easier than the previous nights' exertions but once again, he returned home without encountering anything suspicious. He followed the same routine the next night, again without incident. This was followed by a short debrief by Martinez over the airwaves, with an arrangement for them to speak by phone the following day, as no mention was made of continuing the operation, the following evening.

The next morning, Martinez rang James and before Martinez had time to say anything meaningful, James quickly asked,

"Can we give it one more night Ramon?"

"James, I cannot get the support of the local Police anymore. We agreed three nights and they have other duties to perform. So too, do my own men. I can have my team in place for one more night but tonight is the last night. My boss is on my back. We don't have the available manpower for the next while and this is even after I told him and I am now telling you, that we have had a possible sighting of the suspect. That's all it is though. It can't be confirmed. We have checked the CCTV pictures of a driver of a silver VW Tourareg, which was hired on the morning of the shooting. Enquiries with the car rental company show that the car was hired by someone for three days and it hasn't been returned. This, believe it or not, is not that unusual. However, the contact mobile number given is out of service. In any case, the car has been circulated as stolen. The driving licence number and name don't match up, so we believe it could be our man, or it might just be a criminal attempting to steal a hire car. The picture on the CCTV isn't good enough to say it's definitely him. I am surprised, if it is him, that he didn't go over the Coll, to get into the Valley and avoid the cameras at the toll booths altogether but we all make mistakes sometime. One more night and then I'm taking you out of harm's way. Agreed?"

"Agreed," answered James, reluctantly.

James realised, that this night's run, was going to be the last opportunity to try and flush Boris out, if indeed he was still on the island. He felt it in his water, even before the possible sighting information had been relayed to him. He had a strong gut feeling; a sixth sense on certain things, regarding people and their habits and movements. He tended to be right and this had borne fruit, throughout his previous police career.

This sixth sense had helped him locate a missing child, back in the 1990s, when a family in Bermondsey, had reported their nine-year-old daughter had not come home from a playground, near the River Thames one evening. The family were adamant that this was out of character and a full-scale missing person search was started. At this time, in the area, there had been a couple of abductions and attempted abductions, so no stone was left unturned. The police riverboat was deployed and divers checked a large area of the River Thames. Mobile Support Units were used and local officers did extensive house-to-house enquiries. Other units that became involved, included CID, Scenes of Crime Officers, Dog Handling Units and extensive press releases were issued.

James had been involved from the early stages and he had taken a statement from the mother of the missing girl. He couldn't put his finger on it but he voiced his concerns that something just didn't add up but without any hard evidence to back up his hunch, it didn't 'have legs'. The family circumstances were looked at and both parents had minor criminal convictions for theft-related offences and Social Services had been involved, but not for several years. The home was searched as a precaution and after a week, there was still no sign of the missing girl.

James, was like a dog with a bone. He felt that the family knew more than they were letting on. He didn't believe it to be an abduction, like the recent others. He had a low-level informant, who he approached for any potential information. It transpired that the family had a caravan at Canvey Island, in the Thames Estuary, that they had failed to disclose to police. After James disclosed this information, a subsequent search of that area, revealed the missing girl had been taken there by her parents and was living with her grandmother in an isolated and remote area. All three were involved in a scam, on the back of the previous abductions and had planned to attempt to extort money, by way of donations from members of the public, as they planned to inform the papers they had received notice that their daughter had been abducted but was still alive. All three adults were later charged with various offences and the little girl was taken into care.

He felt in his bones that Ale Boris was nearby. He hoped he was but it didn't stop him from being afraid. He set off on his run that evening with more focus than on the previous three evenings' runs, with the possibility of Ale Boris being in the Valley. He listened, as Martinez did a radio check and James acknowledged he could hear him. He had reached the top of the road and was making his descent back to the village, when, from further back down the road from where he had come, he heard the sound of gunfire. He heard three short bursts of semi-automatic fire and immediately he heard Martinez shout,

"Shots fired! Take cover James!"

He immediately ran to the opposite side of the road and took cover behind a stone wall. He could hear the sound of further shots and the noise of tyres screeching and then, the sound of a vehicle driving off at high speed in his direction.

"Get out of there! Get out of there!" shouted Martinez to James, down the radio.

He realised, that the vehicle heading in his direction, was surely Boris' vehicle. He hesitated for a split second, whether to stay where he was, or to try and make a run for it into an olive grove on the other side of the road. In that moment of hesitation, any chance of moving had gone. Just then, a silver VW Tourareg car came screeching round the bend, just as he stood up. He could see Ale Boris in the driving seat. He had nowhere to run. He could see that Boris had spotted him and was now driving towards him. He attempted to scale a six-foot stone wall by the roadside. He leapt as high as he could and grabbed hold of a stone jutting out more than others and pulled himself up, just as the bonnet of the car brushed past his legs. He could hear the impact of the vehicle as it collided with the wall but it continued on its path and round the corner and out of his sight.

Seconds later, he could hear the sound of two sirens heading his way and he climbed down from off the wall, to see the two unmarked police cars, containing Martinez and his men in hot pursuit of the suspect. James gave a thumbs up sign as they passed him.

"Make your way home James!" demanded Martinez over the radio.

James complied and slowly made his way at a trot down into the village and into the safety of his home. He had been listening to the running commentary of the chase, which was mostly in Mallorquin but occasionally Martinez would update him, in English, knowing he was listening in. It appeared that Ale Boris had driven off in the direction of Sa Calobra and Cala Tuent. Martinez had requested a helicopter, which was finally in the air. Other police were making their way from Escorca but the suspect was driving at over 120 kilometres per hour on the narrow, bending roads. Martinez was able to inform him, that they had spotted the car from their observation points in Fornalutx and had moved in to apprehend Boris, who had been in position with a high velocity rifle with a scope, ready for James' return journey down into the village. Martinez had remarked, that his Kevlar would not have been much use.

The commentary continued, as James sat with his guard, listening in on his police radio. He heard animated, raised voices in Mallorquin and the guard then said,

"He's crashed! He's crashed!"

The police guard then took a sharp intake of breath at another revelation that James didn't understand.

"What's happened now?" James asked, anxiously.

The guard was clearly trying to find the words in English and after a short pause said,

"Boom! Explosion!" whilst gesturing with his hands.

It was not long before Martinez' voice came over James' earpiece.

"James. The fuel tank of the car has just exploded with Boris inside. It may take us some time to put this out and I'm not rushing. He's not Russian either, he's Bosnian!" laughed Martinez at his own joke, before adding,

"Seriously though James, this guy is not going to give you any more trouble. I'll see you later."

The relief of some potential closure struck him. He breathed a sigh of relief and sat down with his head in his hands. He had just been listening to a high-octane, police car chase of a suspect who, had been in the advanced stages of attempting to kill him with a sniper's rifle. The whole escapade had just ended with a car crash and an explosion. It was surreal. He had just listened to something that wouldn't have been out of place on a movie set in Hollywood but this was real and he had been at the centre of it.

He removed his earpiece and took off his running top and Kevlar vest. He went to the fridge and took out a bottle of water and took a long drink. He then slowly walked upstairs and dialled Charlotte's number. He heard her voice say hello and emotions got the better of him and he hung up his phone. His release valve, which had been storing up all his stress for months now, in that moment, had been switched to FULL ON and he found himself blubbering like a baby. Tears streamed down his face and he was almost choking. He wiped the mucus from his face, which had explosively been expelled from both nostrils simultaneously and he tried to compose himself, in preparation to re-dial.

Before he could, his mobile phone rang. It was Charlotte. Taking a deep breath, he answered.

"Hello," he said, timidly.

"James, is everything alright?" she asked anxiously.

"It is now. Sorry, I just needed a moment there. OK. I'm fine now. I just wanted to let you know, the guy that shot Matt, the guy who was after me... he's dead. I'll tell you all about it later but, as long as Martinez agrees, I think you can come home. I would love it if you guys came home," said James, pausing, as he felt himself welling up again.

"OK. We will. We will come over straight away," said Charlotte, with concern.

"Unless you hear differently from me, come back tonight. I'll ring Martinez to confirm he's OK with this but I think with this guy out of the picture, we should be in the clear."

"OK, James. See you soon. The boys miss you. I miss you. Love you," said Charlotte softly.

"Love you too. See you tonight."

James spoke to Martinez, to inform him of his family's home coming and as Martinez was satisfied that Ale Boris had been working alone and the fact that they had pulled his charred remains from the car and he had been pronounced dead at the scene, he was happy with the arrangement. An hour later, Charlotte and his boys returned home and James felt that a vital piece of his jigsaw of life had just been returned intact to him. He felt a weight had just been lifted off his shoulders.

Chapter 11

A Time For Reflection

The sound of Michael Bublé singing 'Feeling Good', emanated from the roof terrace and woke James from a well-needed lie in, the following morning. He could hear that Charlotte and the boys were all up and having breakfast. He looked at the clock, which read 10:23. He had slept right through and Charlotte had obviously filled in for breakfast duties at the hotel. It was Saturday morning, so at least there would be no need to worry about school for the boys. There were only a few weeks left until the end of the summer term for both boys and James was relieved that Reuben had only missed a week and a half, due to their self-imposed exile in Calvia. He lay on in bed and listened to the words of the song, 'Birds flyin' high, you know how I feel, sun in the sky, you know how I feel, breeze driftin' on by, you know how I feel. It's a new dawn, it's a new day, it's a new life for me and I'm feelin' good.' He thought poignantly about the lyrics and reflected they almost summed up his life. The sun was shining, the swifts and swallows were soaring and diving near his bedroom window over the cobbled street below. Perhaps this really was a new dawn for him and his family, after so many recent false ones. He may not have been feeling good right at that moment but he felt better than he had, after the week he had just endured.

The few moments of lazy peacefulness were interrupted by the realisation that there was still little or no hope that Charlotte would want to stay in Mallorca, after everything that had happened. They had deliberately steered clear of the topic the previous night and had just enjoyed some intimacy after their reunion. James was not eager to bring the subject into conversation, as he knew he had no meaningful assurances that he could give her, right at that moment.

He got out of bed and stuck his head around the door to the terrace.

"Morning all," he said in a half-yawn, "I'll be with you shortly."

He availed of a quick shower, got dressed and joined his family on the roof terrace. His breakfast was on the table, waiting for him.

"Oh, this is great! To have you all back and sitting here, having breakfast in the sunshine; just marvellous!" he exclaimed.

Adam smiled and nodded and then returned to his game on his iPad. Reuben was drawing in crayon on a piece of paper, trying to hide his work with one hand.

"What are you drawing Reuben?" he asked, taking a mouthful of cereal.

"I'm not finished yet! You can't look until I've finished it," he said, sternly.

"OK. I'll not look. You tell me when it's finished then."

James finished his bowl of cereal, as Charlotte made some coffee.

"Everything OK next door?" he enquired.

She turned and nodded, smiling.

"Thanks for covering. I really needed that sleep. How are you feeling this morning?" he asked tentatively.

"OK, I suppose. I'm glad to be back. That's as much as I can tell you for now."

"Good, good," said James, not wishing to push his luck further.

"It's finished Daddy!" declared Reuben, holding up a card reading 'Welcome Home Daddy,' with four stick people representing the family.

"That's lovely Reuben. I suppose, I should be the one making you all a card, as it is me welcoming you all back."

"That's right, so I did one for you," said Reuben, as he handed it to James, before saying,

"Now you have to give me the card."

"There you go Reuben," said James, returning the card to his son.

"Oh, thank you Daddy!" exclaimed Reuben, "Look Mummy. Look at the lovely card Daddy has given me. He must be a very good artist Mummy."

James smiled at Charlotte.

"I think we should go into Palma this morning. There is a street food market on in Poblo Espaynol and we could maybe go to Ciudad Jardi and Portixol afterwards. Who's up for that?" asked James, enthusiastically.

Adam gave him a 'thumbs up' sign, without moving his gaze from his game on the iPad. Rueben was oblivious to the question, as he was continuing to draw. Charlotte turned and said,

"I will need to OK it with Monica. She said this morning over breakfast that she might need to leave early, to collect her mother from the airport. Let me see is she can stay until five."

Charlotte left the terrace. James sipped his coffee and was enjoying the peace of the morning. The silence was occasionally broken, by several of the normal sounds they had grown accustomed to, from their location within the village. Firstly, there was the chiming of the village clock on the church, which sounded on the quarter hour. There were also the sounds from various residents of the village, of the animal kind. A donkey brayed with vigour from a nearby olive grove and James could hear the gentle, deep tinkling of bells around the necks of some sheep in the distance, as they walked. The scream of a peacock kept on a small nearby farm, completed the menagerie of sounds. Later in the day, the low croaking of bullfrogs and the chirping of the cicadas would make an appearance. Add to this, the song of the swifts and swallows and the early morning wake up call of a crowing cock and you had a real sense of being close to nature. The backdrop of the glorious Serra de Tramuntana gave conformation of this.

James drained his coffee cup as Charlotte reappeared.

"Right, it's all sorted. We can go if you like."

"I'd like to. Let's go guys. Venga, va vamos!" said James, clapping his hands to gee up his sons into action.

They arrived outside The Poblo Espaynol in Son Espaynolet, Palma, in the late morning and walked towards the castellated entrance. James enjoyed the ambiance of this 'white elephant' when a market of some sort was on, giving it some life outside of its normal opening days, when it was a little lacklustre. It essentially was an open air museum of Spanish architecture, made up of a collection of reproduction houses, palaces, churches and fortresses, all from various regions of Spain, such as The Alhambra from Granada. It had been the brainchild of renowned 1960s Spanish architect, Fernando Chueca Goitia, who had faithfully reproduced over 100 monuments and buildings.

They walked through the maze of little cobbled streets and plaças, admiring the sixteenth and seventeenth century replicas, whilst taking in the sights and smells of the array of food on offer from the street food vendors, who regularly held markets throughout the island. After calling to see Sally, a friend from Soller, who was selling homemade muffins and cupcakes from a much admired, retro Citroen H van, under the name 'Glace Moustache', they made their way to another food establishment, called 'Manduka'. They produced the best gourmet burgers James had ever tasted. Consisting of simple but quality ingredients of Aberdeen Angus beef, brioche bun, rocket, mozzarella cheese and caramelised onions. James found it hard to make do with one but with his goals of weight loss and lower cholesterol still in his mind, he resisted temptation.

It was a glorious, early summer day and the heat was more manageable than the stifling heat of July and August. The family headed east by car, across the city along Paseo Maritimo. There were two enormous cruise ships in port. Adam had spotted that one of them was even sporting its own water park with slides. They then passed the iconic La Seu cathedral and drove into

Portixol, an area once made up of rows of fisherman's cottages, but it was now an upmarket, trendy and bohemian suburb of Palma, running along the Playa de Palma. Even on a Saturday in June, it was proving almost impossible to park. They eventually found a parking place and enjoyed the remainder of the day on the golden sands of Playa de Palma, soaking up the early summer sun. The day was rounded off with tapas at Mercado Gastronomico San Juan in S'Escorxador, a rejuvenated former slaughterhouse, now a trendy location for tapas and ended their excursion with a film in English, at the adjacent cinema.

They returned home to Fornalutx and James carried both boys back to the house from the car, both clearly exhausted by a full day of activities. They were asleep almost before their heads hit their pillows and James retired to the living room and sat down. It had been an enjoyable day and the sort of day he had imagined having in Mallorca, before they had moved permanently to the island. As he pondered their situation, James' mobile phone rang. It was Martinez.

"Good evening James. I just wanted to tell you the news. First of all, I got a call from Matt's doctor at Son Espases. He is being discharged from hospital tomorrow. He has been making excellent progress in his rehabilitation. He is now walking on crutches. He will still need physiotherapy to aid his recovery but they think he will be able to walk unaided in a few months."

"That's great news. I spoke to him during the week and he was telling me he hoped to be home soon."

"The other news is that I have just received notification, that my application for your award has just come back and it has been approved. You are to be awarded The Medala al Merito de la Proteccion Civil! Fantastico!" exclaimed Martinez.

"I really don't know what to say Ramon. I really don't think what I did deserves such an honour."

"Nonsense! Without you, we would not have caught those two robbers and we wouldn't have recovered the money. Also, you helped us in the Daly murder enquiry and without you, we would not have made the arrests of the drug importers, nor seized nearly 10 kilos of cocaine. Then there was Ale Boris. Need I go on? My boss backed my application and he knows people in high places, so my friend, please stop being so humble! You deserve this. There will be a special ceremony in The Almudaina Palace in Palma next Wednesday at two pm. I have posted your invitations today. It is a great honour James. My boss and I will be present and there are four invitations for you, so bring Charlotte and the boys too."

"Wow! I am really flattered. Thank you Ramon. I had better get my suit out of mothballs."

"Out of what?" Ramon asked.

"It's just an expression. Living here, I have had no need to wear a suit but I've kept a few, so it's fine. I had better go and break both sets of good news to Charlotte. Thanks again, Ramon. See you on Wednesday. Adios."

Charlotte was downstairs in the kitchen, when James found her.

"That was Ramon on the phone. Firstly, Matt is coming home tomorrow."

"Oh that's good news. We must go and see him tomorrow evening. I'll ring Jayne to see if she's OK with that," said Charlotte.

"Secondly, you'll need to put your glad rags on and the boys will need to take Wednesday off school, as I am being presented with a medal of honour at a ceremony at The Almudaina Palace, no less!" said James, blowing on his fingernails.

"You're kidding me!" exclaimed Charlotte.

"Yep. Your husband is being rewarded for assisting the Police in the global war on terror, well I mean, helping catch robbers and drug dealers, at any rate."

"I'll have to buy a new dress for this. Is it too late to ring Jayne? I want to tell someone about this and I can ask her about tomorrow. OMG!" said Charlotte, excitedly.

"One thing though Charlotte, please do not put this news on Facebook. Promise me."

"OK. Well not now, at any rate," she replied, lifting the phone to relay her exciting news to Jayne and to make arrangements to see Matt the following day.

The next evening James, Charlotte and the boys drove the few kilometres to Port de Soller. Matt, as expected, had been released from hospital and they were there to see him and his family.

In the aftermath of what had happened, James had resolved to re-kindle his friendship with Matt. After all, he thought, 'how many people these days would take a bullet for a friend? Even though, some of the blame for the discharging of that bullet, may lie at the friend's door.' Still, he felt closer to Matt, than he had before. He respected his bravery or foolishness or whatever it was, to have made him do such a thing. James was resolved not to say anything regarding Matt's past or on his involvement surrounding the Daly murder. Everyone needed a second chance and Matt had certainly proved worthy of his.

Adam and Reuben went to one of the bedrooms to play on an Xbox with Matt's boys, leaving the adults to chat. Matt was in remarkably good spirits, thought James, for someone who had been so close to dying, even making a joke that he had simply stumbled at the crucial moment of the shooting, rather than being responsible for any heroic attempt to protect James. James knew otherwise. As the evening progressed, Matt got to his feet, tentatively, with the aid of his crutches and asked James to bring their drinks and follow him to the rear terrace of their apartment.

Both men sat down alone in the solitude of Matt's terrace, to the rear of the property and well away from their families.

"You know that I owe you my life, don't you?" said James, reverently.

"Oh come on James! Keep it light, would you? Anyway, I told you, I tripped. You just got lucky!" laughed Matt.

James smiled and took a drink of his beer.

"You know our secrets will remain just that: secrets?" confirmed James.

"I know, I know they will," said Matt, acknowledging James' sincerity. "Look, the reason we're out here, is because I've got something to tell you and I need you to do me a favour, since well, now you owe me one," started Matt.

"Oh, oh. This is ominous," interrupted James.

"Firstly, before you fly off the handle, just remember I took a bullet for you and I'm still in recovery."

"Go on," said James, looking uncomfortable.

"Do you remember when I got beaten up at the El Trap racing stadium and I got robbed of all Kusemi's money?"

"Yeesss," said James, slowly.

"Well, let's just say, there was a certain amount of pre-planning and acting involved."

"Pre-planning and acting?" repeated James, looking puzzled.

"Pre-planning, in that I paid a few guys I know, from the fairground in Palma, to play the part of thugs. They overdid the attack on me, if I'm honest. They were only supposed to knock me over. They went a bit far for my liking but it certainly did the trick. What they took was a rucksack full of out of date magazines, not money. That was never in danger. In fact, with Kusemi very kindly allowing me to retrieve his other £100,000 that has bumped up the total nicely."

James sat agog, incredulous as to what he was hearing.

"Now James, I am not a greedy man. I only want what I need and I have added up the total and with the exchange rate being particularly good at the moment, I estimate there is over €1 million in cash. You know, this is money without any real victims. Well, if we discount Daly, Kusemi and Ale Boris, I mean real, law-abiding citizens. The insurance companies will have compensated the bank and the victims of the robbery and the remainder is drug money. If we disclose the whereabouts of this money, it will be simply be wasted by the police or may even be syphoned off by some bad apples. Don't look at me like that! You know you are not all saints in the police. Anyway, I am not sure at this stage, if I am ever going to be able to resume with my sign-writing business. Ladder climbing may prove difficult. So, I propose to keep a third of the money, by way of compensation for my injuries sustained. I want you to have a third…"

"No. I can't do that," interrupted James, "It wouldn't feel right and anyway Charlotte would divorce me, if she found out I had taken a penny of that money, after everything that has happened," he added with passion.

"I won't do this without you James. The other thing is, I want you to take the remaining third to Kusemi's ex, for his son. I think you said her name was Jackie?"

James nodded.

"I spoke to Danny in prison, before he died and it was clear he was passionate about his son and his son's future. It resonated with me and my upbringing; so I feel that his son deserves a chance to get out of that area and make a proper life for himself. I know that he was being sent to a public school and with Danny now gone, that source of income has stopped. I want you to go to Rotherhithe and deliver their share to them. I think Danny was a bad man but it wasn't always that way. I think I owe him this. It will be like a legacy or something. I can't exactly do it at the moment, now can I? Will you do it for me James?" asked Matt.

James sat in silence for a moment, taking in what Matt was asking him to do. He looked at Matt and he could see this obviously meant a lot to him. He felt, that perhaps Matt was feeling responsible for Danny being killed and felt guilty about his son, Mehmet being left without his father's continued financial support, even though that support came as the direct result of criminal activity. James felt that the sentiments around the cause were noble and said,

"I will go to London for you but I'm not taking any money for myself Matt. I can't. I won't. When do you need me to go?"

"Sooner, rather than later. I would really like to see some resolution of this whole thing. I haven't been able to sleep much for a long time. By doing this, it might help in my mental rehabilitation. The physical side, well, I think I can manage that."

"I can go after this Wednesday. I'll go just for a night and catch up with Bam Bam while I'm there. OK, I'll do it. Regarding the money, leave it with me. I may have a way of using my share without me gaining from it. I'm not saying yes. I'm saying, leave it with me. Now, regarding the money for Danny's widow and getting it through security, I have an idea. I had a friend at airport security at Heathrow, who gave me a few tips once. You get me the money and I will buy several rolls of plain wallpaper. The money is high denomination notes, which is good. I will put some interior designer paraphernalia in my suitcase. I will use a water-based paste and stick the notes to the wallpaper, like a designer 'bling wallpaper' and reseal the paper in its packaging. That way, it should not draw any unnecessary attention going through the x-ray scanners."

"Sounds like a plan," said Matt.

"When can you get me the money?" asked James.

"Tomorrow, if you like," replied Matt.

"OK. I'll call for it tomorrow night. That will give me time to get the other bits and bobs and I'll look at flights to London from Thursday onwards."

"OK. No problema."

The evening was rounded off and the following day, James purchased the equipment he would need to smuggle the money into the UK, undetected. He called and retrieved the portion of sterling agreed to be given to Danny's widow, for the continued education of her son, Mehmet. He then took the cash back to his study and spent that evening sticking countless £100 notes to several roles of wallpaper, whilst Charlotte was out for the evening with his sons. Once the wallpaper paste had dried sufficiently, he then re-sealed the cellophane wrapper carefully and glued the ends back together and placed them in a suitcase in a cupboard.

James informed Charlotte that he was planning a trip to London, to catch up with his old friend and former police colleague, Detective Sergeant Wiggins, affection-ately known as Bam Bam, due to his girth. He booked his flight for the day after his award ceremony. He was nervous about trying to take such a large quantity of cash through customs and didn't wish to dwell on the outcome, if he was caught. He felt he owed Matt, whose sentiments he felt were noble, albeit that he would have preferred for the money to be handed over to the authorities. But, he had given his word and he would fulfil his promise to his friend.

Chapter 12

An Unusual Week

James cleared away the breakfast dishes, once the last remaining table of guests had vacated their breakfast table, at Hotel Artesa. Today was Wednesday. It was a big day for him and his family. The boys had been allowed to take the day off school and they were going to watch their Dad being presented with a medal at a beautiful palace in Palma. James had not been told who the guest of honour would be, presenting the medals, but he presumed it would be someone of appropriate importance for such an event. He had received two previous accolades during his service in the Police, for going above and beyond the call of duty but to be receiving a medal, as a civilian in Mallorca, felt very special indeed to him.

A few hours later he donned his suit, having recovered it from the dry cleaners earlier in the day. Charlotte was wearing a new dress she had purchased for the event and Adam and Reuben looked like little pageboys, in their smartest outfits. They set off in good time and were due to meet Martinez in a café, near to the venue.

The event itself, was not as nerve-racking for James, as he thought it would be, once he had settled into the ornate surrounding of the large room within the palace. There were about a hundred dignitaries and other family members of the award recipients and about twenty people receiving awards. Some were police officers and others were members of the public, being recognised for their acts of service. All were Mallorcan, as far as he could tell, except for him. He noted on the order of service, that the British Consul was in attendance and that the medals were to be presented by the President of The Balearics.

A roll-call of recipients was soon underway and he was sixth in the running order and sure enough, it was not long before his name was called out and he walked along the red carpet in the centre of the room, to the front and shook hands with the President, Francina Armengol, who congratulated him in Catalan and presented him with his medal, before both posed together for several photographs. He returned to his seat with his head held high, unable to suppress a broad, proud smile.

He got congratulated by the British Consul and met many of the invited guests, at a reception after the ceremony and had time to give a quick interview to a friend and Soller-based journalist, who was in attendance, for a piece to run in *The Majorcan Daily Bulletin*, a locally based, English newspaper. The day had been an exciting one and his two boys seemed to revel in the attention their 'hero' Dad had been receiving but they were becoming bored, so at an appropriate time, James made his excuses, and he and his family left the reception, thanking Ramon, in particular, for his input.

On the journey back to Fornalutx, the silence was broken by Charlotte.

"That was a good day. I've been thinking... despite everything that you have put us through, I think we should give it more time here."

James looked across at her from his driver's seat and smiled. This was what he had been waiting for. Right at that moment, those words meant more to him than the medal, which had just been bestowed upon him.

"Well, I think in recognition of me now being like Spanish royalty, we should celebrate with a meal worthy of such. Where should we go?" he asked, with a wry smile.

"We haven't been to Ca'n Bouqueta for a while. Although, we could just see if Simon has any tables for tonight at Café Med in the plaça and then we can both have a drink," suggested Charlotte.

"Fine. We'll call on our way past."

A celebratory meal was enjoyed by the whole family at the local restaurant of their friend, Simon, overlooking the picturesque Fornalutx plaça, allowing both Adam and Rueben to go and play with local friends after their meal, within the confines of the little plaça, leaving James and Charlotte to reflect on her decision to stay and put all the unpleasantness behind them. James felt very happy. He had been touched at receiving his award. He had just enjoyed a lovely meal and the vista of the plaça with his sons contentedly playing with local friends, made his contentment all the greater. He would enjoy the evening and concentrate on his other objective tomorrow.

After paying the bill and seeing that Adam and Reuben were still enjoying interacting with some of their local friends, they decided to have a nightcap at Café sa Plaça, before retiring for the evening. It was still only half past nine and despite both boys needing to be up early for school, Charlotte, in particular, was eager to allow them a little more time.

"It's good to see them playing with the local kids, especially Rueben. It is really helping his Catalan. This is what coming here is all about," said Charlotte, taking a seat, as they were both greeted by Jaumo, the café owner.

"Buenas tardes. How are you both?" enquired Jaumo, "What would you like?"

"I would like an Aperol spritz," said Charlotte.

"Para me, un Estrella Galicia, por favour, Jaumo", replied James, practising his limited Spanish vocabulary.

The couple sat, sipping their drinks and watching their sons play 'statues', with several of Reubens friends and a little girl, who appeared to be on holiday, as they had noted, she had been encouraged by her parents, who were sitting at an adjoining table to theirs, to join in.

The two other café bars' tables were more than half-full and there was a pleasant buzz of activity all around the plaça. Some of the villages' elderly residents were still sitting on a little bench on the periphery of the plaça, watching the life blood of any village or town; its people. James thought how lucky these old people were, to spend their remaining days in such a beautiful place as Fornalutx. They had the company of other older people, if not family close by and they didn't need the distraction of a TV screen, when their entertainment was happening right in front of them. In that moment, a certain sadness came over James.

He would have loved to have been able to have looked after his elderly parents within the welcoming bosom of his little village. He had lost his father, shortly before they made their move and his elderly mother had suffered from vascular dementia for several years now and was in a care home. He still visited her throughout the year but did not get to see her as often as he would have liked. He was momentarily uplifted, in recalling that they had been able to come and stay in his house, several years previously, before their physical and mental health had deteriorated and this gave him some succour.

"This was a nice way to spend an evening," he said, smiling at Charlotte.

"Very pleasant," she agreed, trying to stifle a yawn.

"We had better get you home, my lady. Anyway, the boys are back to school in the morning and I've got a plane to catch."

All four wandered up the few steps from the plaça to their street and then home, as James admired how pretty their little cobbled street was and apart from the odd electric light, thought that it probably had changed very little over the past couple of hundred years.

The following morning, Charlotte dropped James off at Palma airport, to catch his flight to Stansted, after completing the school run. Monica was to see Rueben onto the school bus, which took him the short distance from Fornalutx to Soller. James was in a quiet, reflective mood on the journey to the airport. He had enjoyed the previous evening and he felt a little annoyed, that he was having to be torn away from his family, albeit, for only a night. It was the fact that what he was going to be doing had a certain amount of risk attached to it that was troubling him. He didn't want to dwell on what might happen, if he was caught trying to smuggle a quarter of a million pounds in cash into the UK. It would be assumed that the money was being laundered and questions would inevitably be asked by the UK police and later, Martinez. He would, at the very least, have to relinquish his new award, if not be charged with an offence. There was a lot riding on this trip, not just a promise to a friend.

As Charlotte dropped him off, he kissed her goodbye and he wandered into the departure terminal and past the rows of lockers, where he had first encountered the money, which he once again had a proportion of, in his possession. Hopefully, this time, it had been suitably well disguised and it would not bring him to the attention of the authorities. Having placed the rolls of money wallpaper in a suitcase, bound for the hold of the aircraft, he made his way to the Easyjet check-in desk and checked in for the flight and then he made his way to the departure lounge. He thought it might be a while before his bag would be checked but as the announcement came over the Tannoy for his flight to board, he began to get a little more nervous, believing that it would probably be as he produced his boarding card, that he may be detained.

He got in line and soon he approached the air stewardess, who was checking boarding cards. There were no Police in sight. She smiled and greeted James, before waving him through. He breathed a sigh of relief and boarding the plane, he took his seat. He had made an arrangement to meet up with his old friend Bam Bam that evening and he was due to check into The Hilton London Docklands Hotel, overlooking the River Thames, in a more upmarket part of his 'old manor'. The plan was for him to drive his rental car to Rotherhithe and to call at the home of Kusemi's widow, as long as she hadn't moved, in the hope of finding her at home. If she was out, he would call the following morning, before his return flight and if there was still no sign of her, he would delay his departure and would seek further information about her whereabouts from his friend.

His plane touched down, 10 minutes ahead of schedule and he recovered his suitcase from the carousel without incident. He was still nervous and vigilant, until he finally retrieved his pre-booked hire car and headed out of the airport, in the direction of London.

He arrived in Rotherhithe, mid-afternoon, passing by his old police station on Lower Road. It hadn't changed in over 20 years, from its facade anyway. He then made his way to Rotherhithe New Road and to the house where Jackie and Mehmet lived. There were no cars in the driveway but he parked and rang the front door bell. There was no response. He looked through the blinds of the downstairs living room and noted that the furniture looked the same from his last visit there, so he was content that they still lived there. As he was about to ring the doorbell for a second time, a familiar black BMW pulled up and he immediately recognised both occupants.

"What the hell are you doing here?" said an animated Jackie, getting out of the car.

Mehmet, her son walked past him without saying a word.

"Look Jackie, I'm really sorry about Danny. I've got something for you. Can we go inside for a chat? It will not take long. It's in your interests, I promise you," said James, sincerely.

"Alright, but make it quick. I have to work tonight. Since Danny's death, I've had to take a job down The Blue to make ends meet."

"Just a minute. I need my case," said James.

James recovered his suitcase from the boot of his hire car and walked into the house, through the door she had left ajar for him. As he closed the front door, he heard Jackie call,

"I'm in the kitchen!"

He walked into the kitchen and put his suitcase on the kitchen table and opened it. He lifted out the three rolls of wallpaper containing about a quarter of a million pounds and handed them to Jackie.

"What the fuck am I supposed to do with these?" she said.

He took one roll back off her and took the cellophane wrapper off it and unrolled a section of the paper and held it up to her.

"Do you see these notes? They are real. It's the only way I could get them over to you. There is about a quarter of a million pounds here, Jackie. No bullshit. This is real money. This was Danny's and I think it only right that you and Mehmet should have it. The only condition I would make is that you continue to give

Mehmet as good an education as you can, which you are obviously still doing."

James had realised that they had been returning home from collecting Mehmet, from Blackheath School.

"Oh my God! Is this for real? This is brilliant. I could kiss you! You have no idea what this means to us. Since Danny was murdered, that bastard Kingpin has stopped sending us anything. He always was a slimy little shit. He was nothing without Danny. Now, I'm not saying I liked what Danny got up to but he had honour and he always treated us good as gold. It broke Mehmet's heart when he heard about his Dad's death. Even though, thanks to you, he didn't want to see his Dad no more, it still came as a shock. How am I supposed to get this off then?" she asked, looking perplexed by the money on the roll.

"It will take a bit of work. You can either steam them off one at a time or you can put the rolls in a bath of hot water and then dry the notes off. They are stuck on with wallpaper paste."

"You crafty bastard! I would never have thought of that."

"Anyway, I'd better go. I said I'd be quick. I'm sorry about Danny. That was no way for anybody to go. I hope this helps."

"Fank you so much. I promise you that Mehmet will be given the best opportunities. It is what Danny wanted. He loved that boy, you know. He only really continued with what he did, so his son could stay out of trouble, unlike his Dad. On my muvver's life, I won't waste this money."

"I believe you. Take care Jackie," said James, as he left.

He drove the short distance to his hotel for the night and checked in, relieved to have been able to offload his cargo before meeting Bam Bam later that evening. He had booked a table in the ship restaurant that was moored beside the hotel, in order to stay locally. He was enjoying a pre-dinner drink, when his friend arrived at the restaurant.

"Well, well, well! How are you my old son?" asked Bam Bam, greeting his old friend, before sitting down.

"I'm good. Look at you! You've lost weight," replied James.

"Well, I'm off my seafood diet. You know the one I was on. When I'd see food, I'd eat it!" he said, smiling at his own attempt at humour.

James shook his head.

"You look well, really. I don't think I've ever seen you so trim. What's your secret?" asked James, pouring a glass of wine for his friend.

"Yeah, I've stopped eating in Police canteens. That always helps and I've been going to the gym. I've got myself a new lady friend, who I met on a dating website, would you believe, so I'm trying to make an impression. She's actually a Chief Super from Essex."

"Really! I thought you didn't like to mingle with the top brass. Do you call her ma'am when you are out with her?" asked James, tongue-in-cheek.

"Yeah, yeah. Very funny. She's a divorcee and has two teenage kids. Her old man and I were at Hendon together nearly thirty years ago and he was a shit, even then. When I looked at her profile on the dating website, I had no idea of who she was, or the connection with her ex and although it's early days, I have to say,

I couldn't be happier," said Bam Bam, raising his wine glass to James.

"Well, I couldn't be happier for you mate. I know you have had a difficult time since you lost Cathy to cancer, oh, what is it now, ten years ago?"

"Ten and a half. She will never replace Cathy. She was my soul mate. But, life goes on. We all deserve to be happy and I know that Cathy would have liked Jill. Enough of my love life. To what do I owe this honour?"

"I just thought it would be nice to catch up. I never really thanked you properly for what you did for me in Mallorca and since Danny's death I haven't had a chance to speak to you at length," said James.

"Yeah, I appreciated the head's up on that one. I can tell you, that bastard Kingpin is on our radar. There really is no honour amongst thieves, but Danny was twice the man he is. By the way, I have it on good authority that the Russians have put all that to bed, now Danny and Ale Boris are no longer with us. I was sorry to hear about your bit of bother with Ale Boris. I know you quite literally dodged a bullet there, me old mucker. What I don't quite understand, though, is how you came onto the Russian's radar, James."

"It was a bit of a cluster, to be honest. I can't divulge the whole story, simply because I promised someone I wouldn't. Let's just say, that this person did something stupid. Twice. It then got me involved with the Russians, as they thought I had money, which they said was theirs..."

"You're talking about the money Daly stole from Danny? Look, I'm not interested in where the money is or was, as long as you haven't got in over your head," interrupted Bam Bam.

"I haven't. I could quite easily have done so, for a while but I saw sense. Unfortunately, this other person didn't and I've been acting as his shit deflector for some time now. Hopefully that is now water under the bridge and I can get on with running my hotel now, without mad Bosnians trying to top me. Anyway, where are you working now? I tried calling you at the CID office in Rotherhithe but they said you were working in a different department, which is when I rang your mobile."

"I thought I told you when you called. I've gone to SCD7 or Serious and Organised Crime Command. I'm in the Central Task Force, dealing with serious traffickers and gun crime. That's how I got to know about Kingpin and Ale Boris's boss. Look James, I know that they thought that you had money that belonged to them but I only found this out over the last couple of days, otherwise I would have been straight on the blower. I also know that they were then told that you were not involved, by Kusemi. The thing is, these guys don't care about who gets in their way. They are evil, greedy bastards. We need to take them down and a lot of criminal gangs like them. You wouldn't believe what goes on here. I tell you, I will do my thirty years and then I'm out of London. If things go well with me and Jill, we'll have two good pensions coming in and she feels the same: thank you very much and goodnight. Hey, you never know, you might see us over there in a couple of years, but all joking aside, I think it would be too hot for me, especially in the summer, with my fair skin and all. No, a little place down in Deal and my fishing rod and I'd be as happy as a pig in shit. Here I am rambling on and I haven't even asked how

Charlotte and the boys are coping, after everything that has happened. That is some woman you have got there, Semtex, if she's prepared to stay with you, after all the shit you've put her through."

"I know, you're right. She is. To be honest, it was a bit touch and go. I think she had had enough. She just wanted a quiet, normal life for her and the boys, even if it meant uprooting again and leaving Mallorca but just in the last few days, I think she's prepared to give it and me another chance. So here's to the women in our lives," said James, raising his glass in a toast.

"To our women," toasted Bam Bam.

"You are right though, but I think we can finally move on now. It hasn't been easy for them; for any of us but I think we have turned a corner. Anyway, what do you fancy?" asked James, looking at the menu.

A pleasant evening was spent with his old friend and James returned home to Mallorca the following day. Mission complete.

Over the next few months, he ran the hotel and enjoyed a more settled life. The summer season was very busy with guests and he decided to keep the hotel open for most of the winter season but would close for a couple of weeks in November. Adam had not had any more nightmares and his sessions with a counsellor had proved invaluable but they felt were no longer necessary. Reuben was progressing very well at his new school and his Catalan and schoolwork were of such a good standard that he would not have to repeat a year, which had been a worry for both Charlotte and James.

Charlotte seemed to have put to bed, any ideas of moving and was enjoying her walks through the mountains with the walking group and she was continuing with her Catalan classes, in order to assist Reuben with his homework. She was going to yoga classes and had even joined an African drumming class. All of this, on top of being a mum and helping James to run the hotel. At least they could have some respite for a few weeks, when the hotel closed.

It was during this time that James had arranged for Charlotte and him to take a trip to Palma, while both boys were at school. He had initially told her that it was just to do some shopping in Palma but he had to divulge a little more for her to agree to miss one of her yoga sessions.

As they drove into Palma, James parked the car in the underground car park on Paseo Maritimo. He had a surprise for Charlotte and he walked her towards the marina. They walked past luxurious yachts and motorboats, towards a pontoon and then walked along the pontoon itself. Charlotte kept stopping and looking at James and was about to speak but he just put his finger to his lips and said, "nearly there," until he stopped right in front of a brand new looking, charcoal grey houseboat.

"What are we doing here?" she asked.

"Welcome to the new addition to Hotel Artesa," announced James, pointing at the houseboat with his outstretched arm.

Charlotte looked confused. She appeared to be reading the name of the boat.

"Soul Is My Ideal Break. That's a long name for a boat. What does that mean and where did you get the money for this? Are you serious? Is this ours?" she asked, somewhat bemused.

"Firstly, yes it is ours, after a fashion. I had it made by a company called Bert and May and it arrived today. The money side of it, just let's say three kind benefactors put their soul into providing it, or at least their money in it."

"James, are you saying what I think you are saying? That the money for this came from that guy Kusemi? If that's the case, I'm not having anything to do with this, no matter how beautiful it looks," said Charlotte, walking away.

"Wait! Let me explain. Look, we will not benefit from this financially. We might get a few days staying in it ourselves, every so often. I would not be happy to simply use that money for our benefit. What I am proposing is that we will rent it out to holidaymakers for enough weeks to cover the cost of the mooring and to pay for its upkeep. For the remainder of the weeks, I have arranged with The Police Treatment Centres, which is a registered charity and with The Police Service of Northern Ireland, to make the boat available, free of charge, to physically injured police officers and those suffering from Post Traumatic Stress Disorder. It will provide a special place for officers for a bit of 'R and R'. The money that I received, has all been spent on this and it is simply a better way of using that money rather than handing it back for new police cars or whatever. Come on; at least have a look inside. It's fantastic!" pleaded James.

James could see Charlotte was weighing up all the information that he had just given her and was trying to make a decision. It was clearly a moral dilemma for her, as it had been for him. Slowly, she started walking back to the boat.

"So this is like a recuperation centre for injured police officers?"

"Exactly."

"We won't make any profit from it?"

"No. It won't cost us anything but we won't make any profit. I wouldn't have done this otherwise."

"Are you sure we won't find ourselves being arrested because of this?"

"Look, the money was untraceable. We have bought a houseboat, which is providing a charitable service and I have registered it as a charity, so no, we will not go to prison. Come on, have a look!" he pleaded, beckoning her back towards the boat.

James helped her on deck. The gleaming new house boat was almost fifty feet long and consisted of two bedrooms, a bathroom, a kitchen and an open-plan living room and diner with wood-burning stove, for the cooler months and elegantly styled in Scandinavian antique style. There were lime-washed, wooden floors and grey-washed wooden panelled walls with designer, caustic, patterned tiles in the kitchen and bathroom. Up on the spacious deck, was a hot tub and a seating and dining area. Charlotte appeared dumbfounded.

"It's absolutely amazing!" she exclaimed, "I want to live here!"

"I thought we could stay here this weekend to, you know, test it out on our future guests' behalf. You know, purely for test run purposes," said James, grinning, due to Charlotte's reaction, finally.

"Oh, of course, just to iron out any glitches," agreed Charlotte, frowning and nodding her head.

"So, can we keep it?" asked James.

"If what you have said is true and it's for the good of injured police officers and we won't go to prison... then I don't see why not. But I still don't understand the name?" she said, looking perplexed.

"Well, it has clearly got soul, has it not?"

Charlotte nodded.

"It is my ideal break and will be for many others. Three men have died over the past year. Two others, including myself could have died. Despite the disreputable reputations of those who did die and despite the misery that we suffered, I wanted this to be an epitaph to their sacrifice. You could almost say, that from the ashes a phoenix has arisen, for the good of many: this houseboat. It just seemed to make sense and it kind of fell into place: 'SOUL IS MY IDEAL BREAK' is an anagram of 'DALY, KUSEMI and ALE BORIS'."

Charlotte nodded in understanding, if not in agreement with the sentiment. She clearly liked a boat of such beauty and James was just happy to see her smile. It had been a traumatic year for his family and he felt that they deserved to be its first guests. Hopefully, their lives in their little piece of 'paradise found' in The Soller Valley, would run more smoothly from here on in. Only time would tell.

Lightning Source UK Ltd.
Milton Keynes UK
UKOW01f0911090616

275930UK00001B/22/P